Mystery and
More Mystery

A mysterious knife that does its fatal work without the aid of human hands—a murderer who thinks he is Sherlock Holmes and solves his own crime—an embezzler who hides his stolen money and then finds getting it back again is a life's work—a beautiful woman who enters a house on a snowbound hilltop and impossibly vanishes from human ken—these are only four of the unusual and ingenious stories in this book which will delight all readers who enjoy mystery and suspense.

As an added dividend, the author has included a section of Notes at the back, which tell how the stories came to be written and will be of exceptional interest to all students of writing.

Altogether, a fitting companion to Robert Arthur's *Ghosts and More Ghosts,* a very popular book with young readers throughout the country.

Mystery and More Mystery

BY ROBERT ARTHUR

Illustrated by Saul Lambert

Random House New York

TO ANDREW & ELIZABETH,
MY FAVORITE READERS & CRITICS.

Contents

Foreword

This is a collection of mystery stories. But the word mystery covers many different types of story. Detection or prevention of a crime can make a mystery story. So can escape from a grave danger. There can be humor in a mystery story. Magic is certainly a mystery, and so is a story of the magical. Or the strange and unknown can be a mystery story.

In this book I've tried to include samples of several different kinds of mystery stories which I have written. I've included some humorous ones and some that might be a little scary. Short ones and long ones. Some suspenseful. Some strange and colorful. You might call the book almost a mystery sampler.

I hope you enjoy it. And if you want to know how these stories came to be written, and where the ideas came from, I'll tell you in a special section at the back of the book. Where you can skip it if you want to.

ROBERT ARTHUR
Cape May, N. J.
1966

Mystery and
More Mystery

Mr. Manning's Money Tree

At exactly noon Henry Manning, a sandy-haired, amiable young man, closed the grilled window of his cashier's cage in the First National Bank. He picked up his brief case and hat, let himself out of the cage, and strolled toward the front door of the bank. The brief case held a thermos bottle and two sandwiches. Everyone knew that on nice days Henry, the promising young assistant cashier, took his lunch to eat in the park.

As Henry went out the door two men in gray suits at the

rear of the bank exchanged nods, and one started after him, unobtrusively. Henry spotted him almost at once, and his heart began to beat faster. If they had a detective following him it meant they were almost ready to arrest him. It also meant that he had no chance to hide the ten thousand dollars which at the moment was safely tucked away inside his innocent-looking thermos bottle.

Since Monday he had known they were on his trail. By now they must be just about certain that it was Henry Manning who had taken twenty thousand from the accounts during the past year. It was amazing, he thought, how a normally honest man could get the stock market fever and plunge in deeper and deeper, hoping at first for the lucky strike that would make him independent, then for the shrewd guess which would enable him to recoup, then——

Well, the twenty thousand was gone and he couldn't pay it back. So Henry, hardened by now to taking money that wasn't his, had appropriated ten thousand more. But with a detective who might arrest him at any moment at his heels, where on earth could he hide it?

As he reached the park a Lakeside bus was just closing its doors. With a sudden inspiration Henry leaped on as the door slid hissingly shut. Through the window he saw his shadow pound up to the bus stop and look helplessly after them. Henry smiled to himself. That was one problem solved.

But the biggest problem still lay ahead. He had no intention of trying to run for it. He'd take his punishment. Who wanted to spend the rest of his life a hunted man? But he did want to be able to count on the money in his brief case to help him make a new start. How, then, could he possibly hide it where it would stay safe until he had served his sentence and was a free man again?

"Melwood Estates," the driver called presently. "End of the line."

Henry got out. They had stopped at one of the new subdivisions springing up all around the city. A hundred houses, all alike, were ranged up and down slopes of newly planted lawn. He walked away briskly, as though he lived in one of the houses. But inwardly he felt a deep despair. It was all so naked and empty out here, where could a man hide anything? Why couldn't he have had one more day? By now the alarm was out for him, but with one more day he could have——

As if electrified, Henry stopped in his tracks. He had reached a corner. Fifty feet away stood a pleasant little Cape Cod house surrounded by naked lawn. Almost beside Henry there was a deep hole in the lawn, and just beyond the hole a handsome spruce, roots wrapped in burlap, waited to be planted.

No one was in sight. Henry took off his hat, mopped his brow, and as if by accident let his hat drop into the hole. When he bent to get it he slipped the thermos out of his brief case and swiftly hid it beneath the loose soil and compost in the bottom of the hole.

It was all done in twenty seconds. Henry was standing erect, admiring the tree, when a cheerful, heavy-set man with black hair came down the walk carrying a pail of water.

"Just admiring your tree," Henry said, his manner neighborly. "Beautiful specimen."

"Should be," the other chuckled. "They charged me a lot for it because I wanted a big one." He put down the bucket and Henry stepped forward.

"Let me give you a hand," he said.

Henry stayed until the tree was planted and the soil tamped down around it. An attractive young woman with light brown hair came to the door of the little house and watched them. A young couple, not doing too well yet—Henry saw the inexpensive car in the driveway. Mentally he wished them well. As he strolled away, to return to the bank and be arrested, he felt a certain fondness for these strangers who unknowingly had helped him solve his problem.

It was three and a half years before Henry saw the tree again. By then he was heavier, looked older, had a moustache, and had a trade. In the prison garage he had become an expert mechanic.

The tree had changed too. It had grown into a handsome young spruce. And the house had grown also, Henry noted as he strolled by. A two-car garage had been added. The same old sedan stood in one half of it, but even as he watched, a much more expensive car drove in and the heavy-set man Henry remembered got out, looking prosperous. His wife came out to greet him, her brown hair blowing silkily about her ears, a husky baby cooing in her arms.

Good, Henry thought. They had done well. They'd be able to afford a new tree when he dug this one up and—he stopped short in consternation. It had never occurred to him what a big job it would be to dig up a well-grown young tree. This was a bustling suburb now, with regular police patrols, with people coming and going all the time—he could never do it, even at night, without being caught.

Henry gulped and resumed his walking. It looked as if he had outsmarted himself. He'd hidden the money so safely that now even he couldn't get at it.

Eventually he evolved a plan. He'd have to get the tree legally. That meant he'd have to buy the house. Of course, he couldn't buy the house now. He had no money, and there was no sign the owner wanted to sell. But he could wait. For ten thousand dollars he could be patient. They were doing well, their family was growing. Eventually they would want. a bigger house. By then he'd have some money.

Having made his plans, Henry wasted no time. He dyed his hair and, feeling well disguised, got a job at a nearby garage, the one which Jerome Smith, the man who owned Henry's money tree, patronized.

He did his best to become friendly with Jerome Smith, but Smith, who was putting on weight now, was brusque and impatient, as though his mind was on bigger things.

But if Jerome Smith was gruff, his wife Constance was charming. Henry was on duty when she brought her car in for gas and oil.

"You're new, aren't you?" she asked, her voice musical. Henry nodded.

"Just since last week, Mrs. Smith. Shall I check the radiator and the battery?"

"Would you?"

Constance Smith sat waiting patiently, the car radio playing.

"Mozart, isn't it?" Henry said.

"Why, yes. You know music?" Constance looked with interest at Henry, brown-haired and personable.

"A bit," Henry said modestly. "There you are, Mrs. Smith. But I'd like to tune that motor soon. Call someday when you can spare the car for a couple of hours and I'll come pick it up."

"Thank you, I will." A week later she did. Henry tuned the motor until it whispered. When he drove it back she was playing on the lawn with her son.

"This is Peter," she said as Henry gave her the keys.

"Hello, Peter. I wonder, now. Are you a boy who likes dogs?" Peter stared at him with solemn eyes. From his pocket Henry took a pack of pipe cleaners, and with a few deft motions twisted a pipe-cleaner dog with large ears. Peter grabbed it in delight.

"Doggy!" he cried.

"Why, it looks so real!" Constance exclaimed. "Thank you. And thank you for taking care of the car."

"It's a pleasure," Henry said. He went back to the garage feeling a warm glow. It was certainly part of his plan to become friendly with the Smiths so that when they were ready to sell he would be among the first to know. But it wasn't part of his plan to look forward to seeing Constance, to feel somehow dull and gloomy when several days went by and she did not stop in the garage for some service on her car. Nevertheless, it happened. Instead of hoping the Smiths would soon decide to move, Henry began to wish they would stay.

By then Henry was manager of the repair department, and his friendship with Constance, though limited to brief chats while she waited for her car to be fixed or perhaps over a cup of coffee in her kitchen when he went to start the car on a cold morning, was a firm one, important to both of them. They talked about books and music and plays, and Henry knew that Constance enjoyed the talks as much as he did. But because Jerome Smith was away most of the time on business these days, Henry was careful not to let their friendship become something anyone could attach undue meaning to.

Nevertheless, aware that her husband was gradually shifting his business interests out West, he found himself more and more gloomy as he contemplated the fact that soon Smith would undoubtedly want to move his family too. So when Constance, sounding upset, called the garage one morning to ask Henry if he could stop in, he was sure the time had come. His heart was heavy as he drove over.

Constance was pale as she led him into the living room.

"Something has happened, Henry," she said, trying to smile, "and I—well, I felt I had to talk about it to a friend."

"I'm glad you think of me as a friend."

"It's a little difficult to say it. You see——" her voice was almost inaudible "——Jerry and I haven't been close for a long time. He's away so much and even when he's home . . .

well, anyway, he's in Nevada now. He's starting some enterprise out there and he'll be there quite a while. So . . . he
suggests in a letter I got this morning that he might as well
establish residence and get a divorce."

"A divorce?" Henry stared at her unbelievingly.

"I'm going to say yes, of course. Goodness, I certainly don't
want a husband who doesn't want *me*." Her laugh was a little
shaky, but it held back the tears.

Now Henry no longer confined himself to business visits,
but dropped in at the little house whenever he could. He
helped Constance find a job as a doctor's receptionist, and got
the mother of one of his mechanics to become Constance's
housekeeper. Proudly Constance had refused the alimony
Jerome Smith had grudgingly offered her, accepting only the
house and, of course, Peter's custody.

During this period Henry was so concerned with making
sure that Constance and Peter were well looked after that it
never even occurred to him that he could get his money tree
until the evening when, after taking Constance to a concert,
he found himself proposing to her.

He was in the middle of telling her how much she meant
to him when it suddenly struck him that if she married him,
the tree was his. And he stopped, wondering in shame whether
he really loved her or whether he just wanted to retrieve his
hidden money. The possibility rattled him and he stammered,
so that Constance laughed softly.

"Henry, are you trying to propose?"

"Yes, I am! I love you!" Henry blurted out.

Constance smiled at him. "You're sure it's not just because you feel that Peter and I need looking after?"

"I'm sure," Henry told her, and knew that he was. "I love you. I want you to be my wife, Constance, and Peter to be my son."

She was silent for a long moment, studying his face.

"Yes, Henry," she said at last. "We'll be very happy to."

So Henry moved into the little house on the corner and finally became the owner of the money tree. But to him this was the least of his achievements.

Now that he had a gracious and loving wife and a handsome son, what need did he have for stolen money?

Still the money proved useful a year later when the owner of the garage decided to retire. Henry didn't have the necessary cash to buy the business. But he knew where the cash was— in his front yard. So he recklessly signed notes. After all, if worse came to worst he could always pay them off.

A mild depression came along, and there were many nights when Henry strolled in the yard, pausing to smell the fragrance of the spruce, scheming how to keep from digging it up just yet. Somehow he was loath to touch it. In the end he managed.

Meanwhile Jerome Smith's photograph appeared frequently in the newspapers. He had become part owner of a big new hotel and gambling casino in Las Vegas and married a stunning blonde chorus girl. Henry and Constance couldn't have cared less.

They had a daughter by now, Anne. The children grew from year to year.

Henry bought an auto distributorship, relying heavily on the money tree, and there followed many anxious nights when he stood beside the tree in the darkness, thinking this might be the last time he could smell its fragrance. The next day he would surely have to dig up the long-buried money. But each time he pulled through somehow.

From then on business boomed, and they could have lived much less simply than they did. But Henry was saving for what he knew he must do. At last the day came—just such a sunny day as that one long ago when as a young man he had come out of the bank with stolen money in his brief case. His hair was graying now, and there were lines of years and living in his face as he entered the bank once more, carrying a brief case under his arm—the same brief case.

When he came out, the brief case was empty. He had returned thirty thousand dollars with interest to date, and his expression had subtly altered. He went home at peace with the world.

That night he stood beneath his money tree and counted his blessings—a devoted wife, a winsome daughter, a sturdy stepson, a flourishing business, happiness, respect, and peace of mind.

The money he had hidden beneath the roots of the tree had done its work. He could forget it now and spare the beautiful spruce he had come to love. He reached out to stroke its needles.

"You've done a good job, old boy," he said. "You've guarded my stolen fortune even against me. I'll never touch you. You can stand forever."

But one day the following autumn an Atlantic hurricane swung in suddenly from the coast and struck the city. All day the wind howled and the rain beat down. As night came, the fury of the storm increased. The street was littered with branches, garbage cans and debris.

Henry was with Constance in the living room, listening to radio reports of the storm, when the lights went out and the radio was silenced. From the yard there came a creaking and groaning, a heightened scream of the wind. Henry, with an awful premonition, reached the window just in time to see, vaguely through the darkness, his proud spruce topple over, leaving a gaping hole.

He felt stricken, as if a friend had died. Then he realized he would have to find the long-hidden thermos before anyone else came upon it.

He was up at dawn. The storm was over. In his boots and old clothes he scrambled into the hole left by the roots of the spruce.

The rising sun glinted on something bright. He reached in gingerly. It was the silvered core of the thermos—the outer steel covering had rusted away long ago. But the glass core was intact and tightly stoppered. He eased open the cork with his knife and shook the bottle. Two scraps of paper fell out. There was nothing else inside. Just two scraps of paper. He picked them up.

One was an old newspaper clipping. With a shock he saw it was a picture of himself and the story of his arrest for embezzlement. The other was simply a bit of notepaper on which was written in Jerome Smith's thick, jagged writing, *I guessed. Thanks, chum.*

A little dazed, Henry went into the house and sat down at the kitchen table. All these years, the money he had counted on hadn't been there! Within twenty-four hours after he had buried it, Smith had dug it up. With it Smith had bought an electronics firm, converted the business to manufacturing illegal gambling apparatus and from that gone on to the ownership of a big hotel and casino in Nevada, later to become a figure in the national gambling rackets, with illegal interests all over the country.

Slowly the shock of realization passed. It was followed by a feeling of profound and humble gratitude. Life was a curiously complex business. The money he had stolen and buried, but never used, had won him a family, success, contentment. For Jerome Smith it had——

Henry shook his head, and picked up the piece of paper on which Smith had written *Thanks, chum.* Beneath it Henry wrote neatly, *You're welcome.* Then he sealed it in an envelope and addressed it. He didn't know Jerome Smith's exact address these days, but from what he had been reading in the papers lately he judged that if he simply sent it in care of the Federal Penitentiary at Atlanta, Georgia, it would get to him all right.

Larceny and Old Lace

A crossing bell clanged. Headlights of waiting automobiles glinted into the coach car. The train began to slow down. Grace Usher looked up from her book.

"We must be coming into the Milwaukee station," she said. "High time, too. It's nine p.m. We're four hours late."

"Mr. Bingham will be wondering what happened to us," Florence Usher agreed. She straightened her black jacket and tidied her hair. Florence prided herself on her youthfulness— she was 70, two years younger than Grace.

"Anyway," Grace said with satisfaction, "it gave me a chance to finish both John Dickson Carr's and Ellery Queen's latest. My, they were exciting! I do love a good mystery."

"I must read them next." Florence made a note in a small red notebook which she carried in a voluminous leather purse almost big enough to be a brief case. "Did you ring for the porter, Grace?"

"And have to tip him a quarter? Nonsense! We can carry our luggage quite well by ourselves."

"But I thought he would help us find a taxi and tell us how to get to Mr. Bingham's office."

"Florence, please don't be provincial. After all, Milwaukee is only a city. And though we've never been in a large city before, we know a great deal about every large city in the world. Why, my goodness, we each have read more than a thousand mystery novels, haven't we? We know about London from Agatha Christie and Margery Allingham, about Miami from Brett Halliday, about Chicago from Craig Rice, about Paris, San Francisco, New York——"

"Yes," Florence interrupted, "it's true we know a great deal about life from reading so many mysteries—but just the same——"

"Just the same, fiddlesticks! I consider we are fully equipped to meet almost any situation, all due to the liberal education we have acquired through reading mysteries," Grace said. "Now we had better get off this train. Mr. Bingham will be waiting for us—at least, I hope so."

Mr. Bingham was. He had been waiting for several impatient

hours in his dingy office, whose glass door bore the legend E. BINGHAM—ATTORNEY AT LAW—*Real Estate and Insurance*. Now he was chewing mints as he poured tea for Grace and Florence Usher. The tea had been brewed over a hot plate whose sole prior use had been for brewing coffee strong enough to help him over a night-before.

"How thoughtful of you!" Grace said, sipping her tea. "Nothing like a nice cup of tea to refresh one after a long train trip. We broke down, you know, fifty miles west."

"I was worrying about you, dear ladies," Bingham assured them. He showed yellow teeth in a smile, the effect of which was spoiled by his large nose and his small eyes, set too close together. "I feared you had decided not to come to claim your little inheritance."

"We have burned our bridges behind us," Florence assured him. "When we received your letter informing us that our nephew, Walter, had left us his house and furnishings, we sold the lending library we have run since we retired from school-teaching, said good-bye to everyone, and came to stay."

"You see—" Grace's bonnet nodded as she leaned forward— "for seventy years we have lived in a small town. And now we are anxious for broader horizons."

A bit of mint lodged in Bingham's long, scrawny throat. "Quite so. Kaff—kaff—quite so. Er—I thought that as soon as you sold your nephew's house you would return to Kiskishaw and——"

"Heavens, no!" Grace told him. "We want to *live*, Mr. Bingham! We are going to transform Walter's house into a boarding house for writers and artists."

"We'll meet such fascinating, creative people," Florence chimed in. "The talk at the dining table will be like music to our poor, starved ears."

Mr. Bingham set down his teacup with a clatter.

"Really," he said, his tone hollow, "I advise you to sell. The house is run down, taxes are high, the neighborhood unsavory——"

But Grace merely shook her head.

"We will cope," she said. "Now please tell us something about poor Walter. After all, we haven't seen him in the last twenty-five years."

"How did he die?" Florence asked, pressing her gloved hands together in eager interest.

"Well," Mr. Bingham rubbed his high forehead distractedly, "he died of a form of heart failure——"

"I suppose," Grace agreed, "that you could call three bullets in the heart a form of heart failure. However——"

"*Two* bullets in the heart," Florence corrected. "The coroner's report said the other missed by several inches. You see, Mr. Bingham, we read all about it in the Milwaukee paper before your letter arrived. We follow all the crime news. Of course, we didn't know then it was our nephew who had been killed. We weren't very much surprised to find out, though. We always felt Walter would come to a bad end."

"As a boy he used to torment puppies," Grace added. "And he was expelled from three colleges, like his father."

"Our brother Henry, you know. He disappeared years ago."

Florence sipped her tea daintily. "We suspected he was in the penitentiary. But if he was he didn't use his own name. Henry always did have family pride."

Mr. Bingham dabbed at his lips with a handkerchief that was not quite clean.

"Of course," he said. "Very commendable. Well, Walter called himself Walter Smith, and until I found a memorandum among his papers directing his property be left to you I did not know his real name, or that he had any relatives.

"He was—ah—well, to be frank, a man of mystery. His source of income was not—ah, known. His house is a large one on the edge of town, but how he acquired it no one knows. One night last month he was entering his home about midnight when he was shot to death on his own doorstep by a mysterious assailant. The police have been unable to catch the killer or even find a motive."

"I'm sure whoever did it had a very good reason," Grace said, patting her lips fastidiously. "When Walter was young we often wanted to kill him ourselves."

Mr. Bingham mopped his brow.

"Eh, yes, of course," he said. He looked unhappily at the two little old ladies, bright as crickets for all their sober, small-town dresses, their old-fashioned bonnets, and gray hair.

"But again, dear ladies, let me urge you to sell your nephew's house. It is really in a shady neighborhood, tainted by a murder, and I have a purchaser who wants to tear it down and build a gas station, so——"

"No. We intend to live there and run a boarding house for

intellectuals," Grace told him firmly. "Now, Mr. Bingham, please let us have the key and the address and a taxi will take us there."

Mr. Bingham, who had once had an iron-willed aunt, produced the key and wrote down an address.

"There," he croaked unhappily, "I do hope you have a—ah —a peaceful night. I do hope so."

"Why shouldn't we?" Grace asked. "Come, Florence, I'm all eagerness to see our inheritance. I've been thinking of a name for it. Do you suppose we dare call it The House of Usher?"

They rustled out. From the window Mr. Bingham saw them lift their umbrellas and hail a taxi. He groaned, hesitated, then went down the gloomy hall to another door on which he knocked timidly before entering.

Inside, a large man in a discreetly tailored suit lounged in a leather chair, smoking a cigar. The room was furnished with a great deal more elegance than Bingham's and the door bore the legend *Gordon Enterprises, Inc.*

Harry Gordon blew a smoke ring as Bingham entered.

"Well, Ed, how much did the house cost me?"

Bingham mopped his brow again. "They won't sell, Harry."

"Won't sell?" The big man brought his feet down solidly on the floor. "Maybe you didn't persuade them right."

"They're going to open a boarding house called The House of Usher."

Bingham lowered himself into a chair.

"They're tired of hick towns." He sighed dismally. "They

want to reside in a metropolis like Milwaukee and live the life artistic. They're two little old ladies and they have wills of steel."

"You told them about their nephew being bumped off?"

"Yes. I told them the place had a sinister reputation, their nephew was a man of mystery—all that stuff."

"You didn't tell them he was the smartest blackmailer who ever put the bite on Harry Gordon?"

"Of course not."

Harry Gordon scowled. "I wished I knew where the devil he hid those ledger sheets he lifted," he said. "They've got to be in that house some place—he wouldn't have trusted them very far from him. But three times we've been over that house and still we can't find them. If they ever got into the hands of the special prosecutor——"

He clamped his teeth down on his cigar. Bingham used his none too clean handkerchief for another face-mopping job.

"If we couldn't find the papers they'll stay hid. Those two old dames will get tired of that gloomy morgue soon, then we'll be able to buy it cheap and tear it down. There's nothing to worry about."

"Maybe we should rough them up a little."

"No, no, nothing like that! That would really start the cops boiling. Newspapers and the public always go for little old ladies like that. They remind everybody of somebody's mother."

"Anyway, they'll get a scare that may send them running," the big man grunted. "I sent Tiny Tinker to the house tonight for another look around. If they bump into him they may decide to sell, and sell fast. Tiny isn't the kind of guy two little old ladies would care to meet in a dark old house late at night!"

"Well," Florence Usher said doubtfully, "it *is* a big house, isn't it? And awfully dark."

"All houses are dark until the lights are lit," Grace informed her. "Let's go inside and put on some lights."

They picked up their suitcases and went up the flagstoned walk that led from a dimly lit street to the old, brown, somehow sinister house that sat back amid scraggly trees. A shutter creaked and Florence gave a little gasp.

"Please, Florence," Grace said, "control yourself. Every mystery story is full of sound effects like creaking shutters. They mean nothing except that some hinge needs a little oil. Give me the key and we'll go in."

Florence handed her the key. Grace inserted it into a very modern lock in a very heavy front door, and the door opened. This time there were no creaks. They stepped into a hall and fumbled until Florence found a light switch. The overhead light snapped on.

"Well!" Grace said approvingly. "Very nice furnishings. Walter was certainly getting money from some source, though I doubt if he was earning it . . . Florence, what *is* it?"

"I heard a noise," Florence said in a strained whisper. "There's someone upstairs."

"You must not let your imagination . . . There *is* someone upstairs." Grace lowered her voice. "It must be a burglar—

someone who knew the house was empty and took the opportunity to search it."

"Let's leave at once," Florence whispered between trembling lips. "Let's send for the police and—and spend the night at a hotel."

"Don't be a chicken, Florence! After all, we know all about the technique of trapping burglars—it's thoroughly explained in many mystery novels. Remember your Arsene Lupin and Raffles. Besides, it is well known that burglars dislike violence. Every criminal sticks to his trade, and burglars burgle. Follow my orders and we will teach Mr. Burglar a thing or two!"

"I—I'd rather not," Florence objected, but Grace was already tiptoeing toward the stairs. She removed her shoes, motioned to her sister to do the same, and in stockinged feet, only their skirts whispering, the two slowly climbed the stairs.

As they reached the second floor the sound of someone moving about became louder. The sound came from behind a closed door near the head of the stairs. Grace and Florence tiptoed toward the door. Grace looked confident and Florence looked unhappy.

"No noise. Let me peek through the keyhole." Grace bent and put her eye to the old-fashioned keyhole. Inside a light was on. A short, heavy-set man with a face like a dish of scrambled eggs was tapping the walls with his knuckles. Tiny Tinker had once been a heavyweight prizefighter, but not a good one.

"There's a man in there looking for something," Grace reported. "We must get him to come out."

"I don't *want* him to come out!" Florence wailed. "Please, let's *go*."

Grace ignored the plea.

"After reading all those mysteries we certainly know how to handle this," she retorted. "Practically all of them agree that the heel of a woman's shoe makes a splendid weapon. As we wear Dr. Borden's Sensible Shoes, with extra heavy heels, I'm sure we're well equipped. Now I'll stand on one side of the door, you stand on the other. We'll each hold a shoe in our right hand. Then I'll toss my other shoe down the stairs——"

A moment later Tiny Tinker, inside the room, heard a clattering noise. "Rats," he muttered to himself and went on rapping the walls. But the noise was repeated a few moments later (when Florence, after some urging, threw her left shoe down the stairs). Tiny, never a great brain, decided the time had come to investigate. He opened the door and stuck his head out, blinking into the darkness.

"Whazzat?" he asked. Then all the knockouts he had ever suffered came back to haunt him. Even a skull like his was not made to withstand the impact of two heels on Dr. Borden's Sensible Shoes.

Tiny went down for the long count.

"Well, we're making progress," Grace Usher said determinedly.

She looked down at Tiny Tinker, who lay on the floor of the room. They had been able to drag him in but not to lift him onto the couch. So they had stretched him out and with a lot of brightly colored neckties from a rack beside the door they had lashed his legs to the couch and his hands, stretched up over his head, to a handsome cherrywood desk. Snoring on the floor, Tiny Tinker looked like a cannibal's Thanksgiving dinner ready for the pot.

"*Now* can we call the police?" Florence asked.

"Certainly not. Take a look at this burglar. See how well dressed he is. He's no ordinary burglar." (He wasn't. Tiny was Harry Gordon's bodyguard.)

"What of it? He's so ugly it makes me nervous to look at him."

"Florence, I am very disappointed in you." Grace surveyed her sister disapprovingly. "After all these years we've talked about living life and having adventures, and now that we're really doing it you keep wanting to call the police. I *really*——"

The phone, which sat on the desk, rang. It rang again. Grace started toward it.

"But Grace——"

"Maybe it's for us."

"Who would be phoning us? Really, Grace——"

But Grace picked up the phone. "Hello?" she said pleasantly. Then she covered the mouthpiece. "It *is* for us! It's Mr. Bingham!

"Yes, Mr. Bingham?" she said into the mouthpiece. At the other end Mr. Bingham sounded as if he might be breathing hard. He asked if they were all right—if everything was quiet —he just managed to refrain from asking if they had heard any unusual sounds.

Beside him, Harry Gordon was chewing a cigar and growling in his ear, "Tiny just has to be there! They must have bumped into him by now."

While Florence listened in disbelief, Grace assured Mr. Bingham that everything was quiet, the house seemed lovely, and thank you for being so thoughtful. She hung up, leaving Mr. Bingham and Harry Gordon staring at each other.

Gordon swore. "Maybe Tiny left before they got there. We'll give him half an hour to check in. Then we'll go over there and see what's going on."

In Nephew Walter's house of mystery, Florence and Grace were also staring at each other.

"Grace, how could you tell such lies? He could have brought the police and taken away this—this criminal on the floor."

"But we don't *want* him taken away." Grace summoned all her patience. "We have to question him first."

"Question him about what?"

"About Walter's death and what this man is looking for— something Walter must have hidden. My goodness, don't you see? This is a real mystery! We're plunged right into the middle of it. It's a chance we never dreamed we'd have."

"What in the world are you talking about?"

"I mean this is our chance to solve a mystery, like all those amateur detectives we've read about."

"But scarcely any of them were women," Florence pointed out.

"Stuart Palmer's Hildegarde Withers is a woman. Also, she is a schoolteacher. I see no reason we shouldn't be able to do anything she could. We'll start by searching this room."

"Well, all right," Florence agreed, a faint flush in her cheeks at the excitement of the chase. "But first we must scan the room for possible places of hiding."

Together they scanned the room. It was a sort of library-den, with Walter's bedroom beyond. It was furnished expensively—the cherrywood desk, several new easy chairs, a shelf of books (all mysteries), handblocked wallpaper, an Oriental rug. On the desk was an expensive pen and blotter set—which had been ripped apart—and two framed photos. One of them was of a busty young lady. Across it was tenderly inscribed *To Walty with love from Peaches.* The other one brought a tender expression to Florence's face.

"Look," she said. "The picture of you and me with Walter when he finally managed to graduate from high school twenty-five years ago. I confess I've always felt a little guilty about giving him a passing grade in Civics."

"As things turned out, he certainly didn't deserve it," Grace agreed, studying the faded photo of themselves, with Walter, a head taller, standing between them. Walter had had a rather narrow face, with a thin mouth and sharp eyes set closely together. He had had fine wavy hair, however. "I'd forgotten how close together Walter's eyes were. But we were quite good-looking then. Yes, and our figures were hardly inferior to that of this—this female with whom Walter seems to have been so friendly."

"Please, Grace!" Florence cast a scandalized glance down at Tiny Tinker, who was groaning softly on the floor. "It isn't like you to be indelicate with a strange man in the room. Anyway, it proves there was some good in Walter. He did remember us even after all these years. And he thought enough of us to leave us his house. Perhaps we always thought too harshly of him."

"Perhaps," Grace said, her features softening. "In spite of his mischief he always did seem fond of us. But back to business. This room has already been searched. The desk has been ransacked, the chairs examined, the rug taken up, the couch almost turned inside out—the work obviously of this individual on the floor. Perhaps we should make him tell us just what he is looking for."

Together they looked down at Tiny Tinker. His face twitched with the pain of approaching consciousness.

"Florence," Grace remarked thoughtfully, "I wonder if this man killed Walter and now has come back to the scene of the crime to look for something he couldn't find at the time?"

"Killed Walter?" Florence jumped a little. "Then he's not just a burglar—he's a murderer. Grace, we *must* call the police!"

"Did you ever read a detective story where the police solved the case?"

"Well——"

"Of course not. Therefore it's up to us. We must see justice done for dear Walter, even if he was a crook of some kind. This creature is regaining consciousness. We'll question him."

Tiny Tinker opened one eye and looked up at them blearily. Florence shuddered. "What makes you think he'll answer our questions?" she asked.

"Surely one thousand mystery novels have taught us the correct procedure as to how to question a gangster! We can't be polite about it. If brutality is called for, we'll have to be brutal."

"You've never hurt a fly in your life," Florence retorted. "How can you start being cruel now?"

Grace ignored the question. "Sssh! He's opening his other eye."

Tiny Tinker blinked painfully up at them.

"What hit me?" he asked.

"We hit you, young man," Grace told him. "We slugged you with the heels of our Dr. Borden's Sensible Shoes. Now we have your hands and feet tied securely so you cannot take it on the lam, or make a getaway."

Tiny Tinker yanked his arms and legs, found the facts as stated, and looked up at them with a tinge of awe on his scrambled features.

"The Usher sisters," he announced. "That's who you dames must be!"

"We find your knowledge of our identity very suspicious," Florence told him, bolder now that she saw the neckties were going to hold.

"Say, you two better untie me," Tiny Tinker said menacingly, "if you know what's good for you. Harry will be looking for me."

"Florence," Grace instructed, "make a note that this person is employed by someone named Harry."

"Certainly." Florence found paper and pencil in the desk and jotted down *Emply by smne nmd Harry.* A trace of alarm appeared on the captive's face.

"I didn't say nothing!" he protested. "What're you two up to, anyway?"

"It's quite simple," Grace said. "You killed our nephew Walter——"

The alarm on Tiny Tinker's face grew astoundingly. "How'd you know that? I mean I didn't neither, you're crazy."

"Aha!" Grace turned a look of triumph on her sister. "We *are* making progress. This man admits he killed poor Walter."

"I don't!" Tiny shouted. "Nothing of the kind. I didn't kill him and I didn't admit nothing. If you know what's good for you, you'll untie me double quick. You're messing in something that's a lot too big for you."

"Aha!" Grace chortled. "Florence, make a note. The prisoner admits he is part of a large criminal conspiracy."

"Yes, Grace." Florence made a note.

Tiny writhed harder. "I didn't! I didn't admit no such thing! What're you two trying to pin on me, anyway?"

"We are simply solving a crime in the accepted manner— just as we have learned it from more than one thousand mystery novels," Grace told him. "Now young man, who's the Big Brain?"

"Who's the what?"

"The Big Brain. Mr. Big . . . Oh, whom do you work for, stupid?"

"I work for Harry Gordon and don't call me stupid. Who

can tell what you two dames are talking about?"

"Florence, make a note. Prisoner identifies the master mind of the criminal conspiracy as one Harry Gordon."

"Wait a minute, wait a minute!" Tiny almost wept from sheer frustration. "I didn't never say no such thing."

"*Two* double negatives in one sentence!" Florence exclaimed. "Where did you go to school?"

"Where did I go to school?" Tiny blinked. "What's that got to do with it?" Tiny could hold out against a team of expert detectives for 48 hours, but the methods of the Usher sisters confused him.

"Never mind," Grace said loftily. "Now let us sum up. You have admitted you killed our nephew Walter, that you work for one Harry Gordon, that he is head of a vast criminal enterprise, and presumably you were searching this house for something of Walter's which Harry Gordon wants. Now what is it? Dope? Hot ice? Stolen bonds? Plates for counterfeit money? You might as well tell us, for we'll get it out of you anyway."

Tiny stared up at two pairs of steel-gray eyes giving him the same looks that had made generations of schoolboys quail. He shuddered.

"Yeah," he gulped, "I guess you will. Okay, I'll talk. Because you can't do nothing about it, see. Harry Gordon has this town sewed up. So this is how it was——"

Tiny Tinker started talking, and Florence started making notes. Tiny had his eye on the clock. If he could talk long enough, Harry would get there eventually. Harry would know how to take care of two sharp old witches like these, in their black taffeta and sweet-little-old-lady bonnets. Harry would probably put 'em on two broomsticks and fly 'em to the moon.

"So there we have the picture!" Grace said when at last Tiny had finished talking. "Walter was a bookkeeper for this Harry Gordon. Walter stole some records of Gordon's criminal activity. But instead of turning them over to the police, Walter hid them and blackmailed Gordon, who got tired of paying and sent this—what is your name?"

"Just call me Tiny." Tiny sighed.

"Sent this Mr. Tiny to search the house. Walter came home too soon and Mr. Tiny shot him. Since then no one has been able to find the incriminating documents. They're still somewhere in the house."

"Which must be why Mr. Bingham tried to discourage us from coming here!" Florence exclaimed. "He's in it too!"

"And now we are on the point of smashing this criminal ring!" Grace breathed, her eyes shining. "What joy, Florence, what a triumph! Even Nero Wolfe would be proud of us. All we have to do is find those hidden papers, turn them over to the special prosecutor whom the governor has appointed, and Harry Gordon, Mr. Bingham, Mr. Tiny here, and many other nefarious individuals will be incarcerated."

"Huh?" Tiny wrinkled his brow. But Florence looked a little doubtful.

"How can we hope to find the missing papers if they couldn't?" she asked. "I still say we should call in the police."

"Florence, you have a negative attitude. First we have to think the same way as Nephew Walter did. We must put ourselves in his place. Suppose *we* were blackmailers—where would *we* hide incriminating documents?"

"Well——" Florence knit her brows.

"How large are these documents?" Grace asked Tiny.

"Size of a ledger page. Walter got away with about twenty pages."

"Big enough to fill a brief case," Grace mused. "Now let me think. If I were Walter——"

"I think——" Florence began, but a voice from the door interrupted her and made both sisters whirl around with little eeeking sounds.

"Please go right ahead, ladies. But you don't mind if I come in?"

Harry Gordon advanced into the room, puffing on his cigar. Mr. Bingham danced nervously behind him. Harry Gordon came toward Grace and Florence like a truck about to crush two small gray kittens. He stopped and fixed them with a sardonic glance.

"Well, ladies, you've had a ball with my boy Tiny, haven't you? But the party's over now. This is the end of the line. Sit down in those two chairs until Ed and I get Tiny untied. Then we'll decide what to do with you!"

Tiny Tucker, released from the neckties, sat gratefully in a corner. Harry Gordon sat back in one of the easy chairs and pointed his cigar at Grace and Florence, who were huddled on the sofa beyond the desk, subdued but still defiant, like two ruffled hens.

"They made Tiny talk," Gordon rumbled. "I say we ought to put them in cold storage."

"No, no, Harry," Mr. Bingham urged, nervously rubbing his forehead. "Please believe me, what they know would never stand up in court. And as I said before old ladies like these are dynamite. Harm them and the newspapers would jump right off the presses screaming. Every fix you have in would come unstuck. Believe me, Harry, whatever you do, don't ever lay a finger on a sweet little old lady."

"Then what do you suggest?" Harry glared broodingly at the sisters.

"Get them out of town and make sure they never come back."

"My way, they'd be sure never to come back."

"If you think you can intimidate us, you're very much mistaken!" Grace bristled. Florence turned on her furiously.

"He is not mistaken. He *has* intimidated us. Anyway, he's intimidated *me*. And I'm willing to make a bargain with him."

A flicker of interest showed in Harry Gordon's black eyes.

"What kind of a bargain, sister?"

"You want this house because it has certain papers hidden in it. All right, we'll sell you the house, just as it is, and you can find the papers for yourself."

"Go on."

"We'll take a trip around the world, leaving as soon as we have the money."

"Florence, I will not bargain with criminals!" Grace cried.

"Be quiet, Grace. You've been the boss up until now. Well, now I'm in charge. Mr. Gordon, how about it?"

"Pay 'em off and get rid of 'em," Bingham pleaded. "We'll find the papers if we have to tear the house down."

"I dunno." Harry Gordon puffed a cloud of smoke. "It'd be cheaper just to bury them."

"We wouldn't stay buried, do you hear?" Florence told him. "We'd—we'd rise up and haunt you."

"I wouldn't be surprised if you did at that," Harry Gordon said. "All right, I'll give you ten thousand in cash for the house, and you leave town tonight."

"Fifteen!" Florence retorted.

"Why, this house is worth at least twenty thousand dollars!" Grace said in great indignation.

"You're in no position to bargain, lady," Harry Gordon said. "All right, fifteen thousand."

"In cash. And you drive us directly to the station," Florence stipulated.

"A deal. We'll pick up the cash at my office. Tiny!"

"Uh—yes, boss?"

"These old—these ladies didn't find those papers before I got here, did they?"

"No, boss. They haven't touched nothing—nothing but me, that is. They spent the whole time questioning me." Tiny rolled his eyes. "Lucky they ain't on the Force."

"All right, let's go. Tiny, stay here. Don't leave this house until you find what I want. Or I'll call in the wreckers and tear it down to the foundations."

"Right, boss."

"Just one thing." Florence stood up. The set of her chin was determined. "We have nothing to read on the train. We prefer mysteries. We'd like to take two of Walter's books with us."

"Oh, you would, would you?" Harry Gordon's tone was silky. "Which two do you have in mind?"

"Those at the end of the shelf—the two green ones."

"Sure. Hand them over to me, Tiny." Gordon held the books in his hand while his eyes searched Florence's face. "You're smart, sister. You figure Walter microfilmed the papers and hid them in these books, huh? Ed, help me search the—" he read the titles—"*The Collected Works of Edgar Allan Poe, Volumes One and Two.*"

He and Ed Bingham painstakingly demolished the two old books. They cut open the covers, slit the bindings, riffled through the pages. Finally, looking peevish, Harry Gordon handed the wreckage of the two books to Florence. She opened her voluminous purse and dropped them inside.

"Come on, let's get going," Gordon growled. "I'm tired of you two and your ideas. I guess you did just want something to read. But if I thought you were playing games with me——" He glared at them, then led the way to the door. "Come on, there's a midnight train."

A crossing bell clanged. Headlights of waiting automobiles glinted into the car. The train began to pick up speed.

"Just midnight," Grace said in their Pullman compartment, her tone discontented. "Florence, do you realize we were in

Milwaukee only three hours?"

"But my, they were exciting hours." Florence yawned. "Really, we must go to bed. We need our sleep."

"How can you expect to sleep after having sold out to a gang of thugs and cutthroats? I certainly won't. Why, we've let Walter's murderers go free, and for just a few thousand dollars!"

"Walter was always a rapscallion," Florence answered. "I certainly did not intend to lose my life over him."

"Just the same, nothing like this ever happened in *any* of the books we have read. I feel mortified."

"I don't think you should, Grace. Remember, we have those two books of Walter's, don't we?" Florence drew out the two volumes of Poe's Works and put them on her sister's lap.

"What good are they?" Grace objected. "The criminals searched these books thoroughly. They didn't find the papers or microfilms in them."

"Because they aren't there. Only the clue is there."

"What clue?"

"You said we must think like Walter. Well, we introduced him to Poe as a boy, didn't we? We gave him these two volumes, in fact. That he still kept them showed me he was still fond of Poe, and that gave me the clue to his thinking."

"You're talking in riddles," Grace said fretfully.

"Not at all. In one of these volumes, *The Purloined Letter* comes right after our favorite—and Walter's—*The Fall of the House of Usher*."

"Oh." Enlightenment began to spread over Grace's face.

"The story about hiding the valuable document inside an old envelope that was left out in plain sight!"

"Exactly. So——" Florence reached deeper into her capacious purse and pulled out a framed photograph—the one which showed herself, Grace, and Walter. Less than an hour before it had stood on Walter's desk.

"Walter had as much sentiment as a rattlesnake," she said. "Why should he keep a picture of himself with us? Only because a picture of yourself and two maiden aunts is about as unsuspicious as anything can be. Nobody gave it a second thought."

"But how did you get it?" Grace asked. "I didn't see you take it."

"In the confusion when Mr. Gordon and Mr. Bingham were bending over to untie Mr. Tiny, I just slipped it into my purse. Now if my analysis is correct, all we have to do is open it up and inside, in back of our picture, we shall find microfilms of the documents which will send Mr. Harry Gordon and all the others to the state penitentiary. Now, Grace, let us look."

The microfilms were there.

"Ellery Queen would be proud of you," Grace said, for she was never one to deny credit where credit was due. "Hercule Poirot would be proud of you. Perry Mason and Lord Peter Wimsey would be proud of you. The Mystery Writers of America would be proud of you, for Edgar Allan Poe is their patron saint."

"Thank you," Florence said, smiling shyly. "In New York we must plan to attend one of their monthly meetings. I feel sure we will be eligible to join as associate members. After that we will take the boat——"

"What boat?" Grace demanded.

Florence looked surprised.

"Why, the boat to London, of course! We have fifteen thousand dollars, so we are going to take a trip around the world—and our first stop will be London."

"London!" Grace sat erect. "The London of Sir Henry Merrivale and Albert Campion! The London of Scotland Yard! Who knows what adventures we may encounter on the foggy London streets? We may be able to help Scotland Yard bring to justice a criminal who would otherwise evade its clutches!"

Her eyes focused on a distant unseen spot. Her voice became dreamy. "Perhaps we can even rent a furnished room on Baker Street!"

The Midnight Visitor

Ausable did not fit any description of a secret agent Fowler had ever read. Following him down the musty corridor of the gloomy French hotel where Ausable had a room, Fowler felt let down. It was a small room, on the sixth and top floor, and scarcely a setting for a figure of romantic adventure. But Ausable, in his wrinkled business suit badly in need of cleaning, could hardly be called a romantic figure.

He was, for one thing, fat. Very fat. And then there was his accent. Though he spoke French and German passably, he had never altogether lost the New England twang he had brought to Paris from Boston twenty years before.

"You are disappointed," Ausable said wheezily over his shoulder. "You were told that I was a secret agent, a spy, dealing in espionage and danger. You wished to meet me because you are a writer, young and romantic. You envisioned mysterious figures in the night, the crack of pistols, drugs in the wine.

"Instead, you have spent a dull evening in a French music hall with a sloppy fat man who, instead of having messages slipped into his hand by dark-eyed beauties, gets only a prosaic telephone call making an appointment in his room. You have been bored!"

The fat man chuckled to himself as he unlocked the door of his room and stood aside to let his discomfited guest enter.

"You are disillusioned," Ausable told him. "But take cheer, my young friend. Presently you will see a paper, a quite important paper for which several men have risked their lives, come to me in the next-to-the-last step of its journey into official hands. Some day soon that paper may well affect the course of history. In that thought there is drama, is there not?"

As he spoke, Ausable closed the door behind him. Then he switched on the light.

And as the light came on, Fowler had his first authentic thrill of the day. For halfway across the room, a small automatic in his hand, stood a man.

Ausable blinked a few times.

"Max," he wheezed, "you gave me a start. I thought you

were in Berlin. What are you doing here in my room?"

Max was slender, a little less than tall, with features that suggested slightly the crafty pointed countenance of a fox. There was about him—aside from the gun—nothing especially menacing.

"The report," he murmured. "The report that is being brought you tonight on Russia's new missiles. I thought it would be safer in my hands than in yours."

Ausable moved to an armchair and sat down heavily.

"I'm going to raise the devil with the management this time, and you can bet on it," he said grimly. "This is the second time in a month somebody has gotten into my room off that confounded balcony!"

Fowler's eyes went to the single window of the room. It was an ordinary window, against which now the night was pressing blackly.

"Balcony?" Max said, with a rising inflection. "No, a passkey. I did not know about the balcony. It might have saved me some trouble had I known."

"It's not my balcony," Ausable said with extreme irritation. "It belongs to the next apartment."

He glanced explanatorily at Fowler.

"You see," he said, "this room used to be part of a large unit, and the next room—through that door there—used to be the living room. *It* had the balcony, which extends under *my* window now.

"You can get onto it from the empty room two doors down— and somebody did, last month. The management promised me to block it off. But they haven't."

Max glanced at Fowler, who was standing stiffly a few feet from Ausable, and waved the gun with a commanding gesture.

"Please sit down," he suggested. "We have a wait of half an hour at least, I think."

"Thirty-one minutes," Ausable said moodily. "The appointment was for twelve-thirty. I wish I knew how you learned about that report, Max."

The other smiled without mirth.

"And we wish we knew how it was gotten out of Russia," he replied. "However, no harm has been done. I will have it back—what is that?"

Unconsciously Fowler, who was still standing, had jumped at the sudden rapping on the door. Ausable yawned.

"The gendarmes," he said. "I thought that so important a paper as the one we are waiting for might well be given a little extra protection tonight."

Max bit his lip in uncertainty. The rapping was repeated.

"What will you do now, Max?" Ausable asked. "If I do not answer, they will enter anyway. The door is unlocked. And they will not hesitate to shoot."

The man's face was black as he backed swiftly toward the window; with his hand behind him he flung it up to its full height, and swung a leg over the sill.

"Send them away!" he rasped. "I will wait on the balcony. Send them away or I'll shoot and take my chances!"

The rapping on the door became louder. And a voice was raised.

"M'sieu! M'sieu Ausable!"

Keeping his body twisted so that his gun still covered the fat man and his guest, the man at the window grasped the frame with his free hand to support himself as he rested his weight on one thigh, then swung his other leg up and over the sill.

The doorknob turned. Swiftly Max pushed with his left hand to free himself from the sill and drop to the balcony outside. And then, as he dropped, he screamed once, shrilly.

The door opened and a waiter stood there with a tray, a bottle and two glasses.

"M'sieu, the cognac you ordered for when you returned," he said, and set the tray upon the table, deftly uncorked the bottle, and retired.

White-faced, Fowler stared after him.

"But—" he stammered, "the police——'

"There were no police." Ausable sighed. "Only Henri, whom I was expecting."

"But won't that man out on the balcony——" Fowler began.

"No," Ausable said, "he won't return. You see, my young friend, there is no balcony."

The Blow from Heaven

Dr. Albert Clane held up the folded sheet of paper he had taken from the envelope and turned to his guest.

"Do you believe in magic, Oliver?" he asked.

His plump friend, Oliver Dace, looked up from his third breakfast egg.

"Of course I do," he replied.

"I mean black magic, voodoo magic," the doctor explained.

His guest looked inquisitive, but did not stop eating.

"There are many different kinds of magic," he said between

mouthfuls, "and I believe in all of 'em. Only some more than others, naturally. What brings the subject up?"

"We're invited to hear an expert on primitive black magic tonight. Professor Kohn, of the Anthropology Department at Queen City College. He returned a few months ago from an expedition to Africa."

Oliver Dace polished off the egg and started on the last slice of toast.

"The one you were telling me about?" he asked. "The one who was adopted when he was a boy by this—this——"

"Madame Fage." Dr. Clane nodded. "She was a wealthy society woman at the time. Now she's still wealthy, but no longer society.

"She's made herself the most disliked woman in this little town. But those who are invited to the affairs when she shows off Professor Kohn always go. The man is a great showman and they're always entertained. He's given us some pretty scary stuff at times.

"She's my best patient, incidentally. Oh, she's healthy enough, in spite of her age, but likes to imagine she's sick. Always afraid she's on the point of dying. Which, I must admit, many people wish she would. Kohn——"

Oliver finished the toast, wiped his lips, and contentedly lit a cigarette.

"You've got a grand cook, Albert," he interrupted. "I think I'll stay with you a while. What were you saying about Kohn?"

"Kohn," Dr. Clane remarked, getting his hat and bag,

"probably wishes she would really catch one of the fatal illnesses she's always imagining is coming on. She finances his expeditions for the reflected glory they bring her. Otherwise she keeps the purse strings very tight.

"If he were a little less intelligent, I'd have looked for him to try his hand at eliminating her before now. But he knows he'd be suspected if anything went wrong, so he takes good care of her. . . . Then you'd like to attend tonight? Here's the invitation."

His plump guest picked up the invitation from the table, and read: " 'Professor Natzof Kohn will speak on his recent investigation of Death Worship in Africa.' That, I should like to hear! You may not have faith in magic. It happens that I do."

"I didn't say Kohn can *do* magic," Dr. Clane said testily, his hat on, his hand on the doorknob. "Though for all I know, maybe he can. All right, I'll phone to say I'm bringing you. . . . Looks like it's blowing up to a storm," he remarked, as he opened the door and let in a gust of wind.

By evening the wind had blown up a storm. The night was black and warm and sultry, with lightning flashing in sheets near the horizon. The first drops of rain fell as Dr. Clane, with Oliver Dace beside him, drove up the gravel driveway of the Fage house.

It was a low, dark building, squatting like a spider among spindly pines, and the inside was scarcely more cheerful, Oliver decided, gazing speculatively about him as he stood in the rear of a big, dimly lit living room. He had been introduced briefly

to Professor Natzof Kohn, who had shaken hands with cold
and aloof disinterest, and to Madame Fage, who had gushed
over him when Dr. Clane toyed lightly with the truth by calling
him "my very distinguished friend from New York—of course
you've heard of him—Oliver Dace, the famous traveler and
writer."

It had been the right note to take with the old lady. Since
they had arrived late, a case having kept the doctor busy until
the last moment, introductions to the others had been deferred.
There were ten or a dozen guests, and they were huddled
as if for company in a nervous little group at the other end of
the room.

The group was dominated by Natzof Kohn, a tall man with
a dead-white face and a hawk's nose between two deep-set
eyes. Kohn was standing beside the little old woman. Madame
Fage, a withered and witchlike woman in a black dress and
high, white lace collar, her shrunken hand resting heavily on
a chair arm, was talking in a shrill voice, imperiously addressing
them all at once, letting no one's attention stray.

". . . and dear Natzof has some of the most thrilling things
to tell you——"

Oliver gazed around the room. It was paneled in dark wood
that soaked up most of the faint light from the two or three
lighted wall lamps. A dozen or so chairs of varied pattern, but
all old, were arranged before a small white screen, and a table
held a moving picture projector, set up and ready.

A servant in dingy livery, moving like a shadow about the
room, finished arranging the chairs for the little audience. A

woman in white, evidently a nurse, entered and took a seat quietly at the rear of the room. Oliver saw Dr. Clane whisper to the old woman, and immediately she turned to Professor Kohn.

"I think we can begin now," the tall man said, in a voice low but vibrant.

The little knot of people hastily untied itself. The dozen or so townsfolk—stoutish women and baldish men—stumbled into seats. Dr. Clane rejoined his friend.

"I told her," he chuckled, "not to overtax her strength. That's the only way to keep her quiet."

As he sat down beside Dace in the last row of chairs he indicated the people in front of them.

"The cream of Queen City society," he said. "The ones she always invites. There's the mayor and his wife, the local banker and his. That large and solemn man is Chief of Police Hoff."

The room was expectantly silent now, and in the silence the rumble of thunder outside was loud. Professor Kohn assisted Madame Fage into a large armchair, then faced them all.

"It gives me great pleasure," he said, in his voice a note of sardonic contempt that went over the heads of his audience, "to exhibit to my friends the interesting things which I happened upon in my research among savage tribes."

He paused to smile, as if at some thought of his own, then continued.

"On this last trip I penetrated into some little-known tribes on the west coast of Africa. The trip did not prove of major importance, it is true——"

"Natzof!" the little old woman shrilled.

"Yes, Madame Fage?"

"Natzof, that trip cost me ten thousand dollars! Do you dare stand up there now and say 'It did not prove of major importance'?"

Professor Kohn smiled, but his eyes were unreadable.

"Ah, Madame Fage," he murmured, "I was about to add that I feel sure a further study of that territory will reveal something highly important."

"Humph! Another expedition on my money, I suppose?"

"I trust," Kohn said silkily, "that your generosity will make it possible for me to continue my work."

"Perhaps," Madame Fage snapped, "and perhaps not."

Kohn bowed slightly, and continued.

"We landed at the coast and made our way inland——"

He continued with his talk, but Oliver Dace found he was not listening to the words. He was studying the man himself. Kohn's voice was rich and vibrant and perfectly modulated. In a few deft words he painted such a setting of African night with drums beating in the distance and unknown horrors lurking in the dark that the rest of his listeners, to judge by their expressions, were almost literally there.

Kohn might have been an actor, playing upon the emotions of his audience. And gradually Oliver began to wonder if that were not exactly what he was doing. In that dim room, occasionally lit by the reflection of lightning through the drawn shades, his voice ran through the muttering and grumbling of the thunder with hypnotic insistence.

". . . the religion of these villagers is a worship of death," he was saying, his eyes bright and unwinking as he stared at his little audience. "These savages visualize death as an actual devil. To die is to pass over into a land ruled by him. . . ."

The tension that had built up in the room was electric. It was an actual relief when the spell was broken by Madame Fage's shrill, frightened voice.

"Natzof! Natzof! Stop this instant!" she cried.

"Like so many useless people," Clane whispered to Oliver, "she dreads the thought of dying. She cannot stand to have death even mentioned."

"I am sorry," Kohn apologized. "I was forgetting the subject is unpleasant to you, Madame Fage."

"You were not, Natzof!" the old lady shrilled at him. "You were deliberately frightening me."

Professor Kohn shook his head gently, a malicious gleam in his eyes.

"I am sorry," he repeated. "I will show the motion pictures of the trip now."

"I don't care what you do, Natzof!" she snapped. "I am going to bed now. But don't think you have frightened me away. You haven't. I'm just tired. And in the morning I shall certainly have something to say to you."

Kohn nodded.

"Nurse," he said. The woman in the nurse's uniform appeared from the rear of the room. Professor Kohn took hold of one of the old woman's arms and helped her from her chair. The nurse took her other arm, and together they assisted her from the room. Oliver watched them cross the hall and enter a room on the far side; a dimly lit room, the interior of which showed for a brief moment before the door closed.

The little audience stirred.

"Isn't he thrilling?" a woman whispered excitedly. "He simply terrifies me."

Oliver turned to Dr. Clane.

"Something is happening, Albert," he said, "which I do not understand."

Clane looked puzzled. "What do you mean?" he asked.

"Professor Kohn is talking gibberish. No religion such as he is describing exists. I believe he is deliberately trying to frighten these people."

"But—but why?" the doctor asked. "Unless it's a joke——"

"I do not think it is a joke. But I may be wrong. We can only wait and see."

They had not heard him enter, but they knew Professor Kohn was in the room by the sudden silence. Oliver looked up. Kohn was smiling down at them.

"Doctor," he said softly. "Madame Fage wants to see you. Could you step in?"

He took his place in the front of the room again. Clane, with a muttered word to Oliver, slipped out.

"I am sorry Madame Fage had to leave us," the tall man apologized. "She insists you all remain, however. Coffee and cake will be served presently. Or I can stop the lecture now, if you are bored."

There were protests from his audience.

"*Do* tell us some more," gushed the woman Oliver had heard claiming to be terrified. "We're all simply thrilled."

The professor smiled and took an object from a box on the table.

"If you insist," he said agreeably. "Now, here——" He turned the object to the light. Steel flashed. "Here is a rare ceremonial knife. I estimate its scientific value at several thousand dollars. It is one of the only two of its kind ever to be brought out of Africa. The other I have presented to Madame Fage."

The audience was properly impressed, and Oliver Dace heard the women murmuring among themselves. Kohn handed the knife to the nearest man, who hastily passed it back to Oliver.

Oliver turned the weapon over curiously. It had a wooden handle, and a broad, hard-steel blade nearly a foot long, wide and heavy. Obviously of European manufacture. He guessed it to be a trading knife of early days. Native workmen had embellished it with crude designs.

Oliver, glancing away from the knife, saw the door to Madame Fage's bedroom open. Dr. Clane came out, followed by the nurse. She closed the door behind her, and they both came in and took seats in the living room.

"We've gotten the old lady to bed," Clane whispered, as he slipped into his seat beside Oliver. "I gave her a strong sedative. Her nerves were badly shaken up. Between the storm and Kohn's little talk——"

"We can have more light, now that Madame Fage has

retired," Kohn interrupted himself to remark. "The dimness, of course, was because strong light hurts her eyes."

He stepped to the wall and snapped a switch. More wall lights sprang on, partly relieving the gloom. Then he stepped back to his place and picked up the knife Oliver had returned to the table.

"I hope no one will accuse me of being theatrical and choosing a night such as this to invite you all here," he said pleasantly, his teeth gleaming. "But the truth is, thunderstorms are greatly feared by the Dambongi savages.

"When a witch doctor has placed the curse of death upon a victim, he waits until a thunderstorm is brewing. Then he places one of these knives where the victim will find it. It is a superstition that Death walks abroad, unseen, when a storm is raging. Death approaches the man the witch doctor has cursed, and causes him to drive the blade into his own breast. Death then takes his spirit back to the Land of Shadows when the storm is over."

He paused to smile again, and the smile was sinister.

"But some of the natives," he went on, "believe that the knife itself is given power by the witch doctor's magic—power to move itself from its hiding place and to plunge itself into the victim's breast with no human hand touching it. They call it a 'devil knife' and insist than an evil force enters the blade and resides there. You may laugh if you wish, but I myself have seen strange things——"

A terrific crash of thunder interrupted him. The lights flickered and almost went out. Oliver Dace saw the man ahead of him start violently, and some woman uttered a little scream. Oliver's lips were tight. What the man was saying was pure invention. And Oliver could not fathom his purpose.

And then, suddenly, he knew. For he saw the nurse cross the room hurriedly and enter Madame Fage's bedroom, no doubt to see if the lightning bolt had frightened the old woman. An instant after the nurse entered the room she screamed.

Oliver was the first man into the room, and he saw why she had screamed. Crumpled on the floor beside her narrow bed, the wooden handle and half the blade of a great knife standing straight up from her breast, was the body of Madame Fage.

No one had entered that room since the nurse and Dr. Clane had left, or Oliver would surely have seen them. But there the old woman lay, curled where she had fallen beside the bed, half the bedclothes draped over her as if she had pulled them with her as she fell, her hands convulsively grasped about the knife.

White-faced, the nurse clung to Oliver's arm. Dr. Clane stooped over the body.

"She was alive when I left her!" the nurse gasped.

"I am sure of that," Oliver said soothingly. "We do not doubt you."

Dr. Clane rose from his examination of the dead woman and looked at them—at the terrified nurse, at Oliver Dace, pink-cheeked and perplexed, at Professor Natzof Kohn, who was quite calm, and at Chief of Police Hoff. That large and solemn gentleman, whom Clane had pointed out earlier to Oliver, was wide-eyed and pale. The rest had been herded back into the living room.

"Dead!" Clane said. "The blade reached her heart."

"Someone," Chief Hoff said thickly, "got into the room while we were listening to the professor."

"No one," Oliver Dace said quietly, "entered the room after the nurse left. I was sitting where I could see the door the entire time."

"She was alive when I left her," Nurse Minor repeated hysterically. "She spoke to me. She said——"

"No one doubts you, Miss Minor," Kohn interrupted pleasantly.

Chief Hoff looked all about the room. It was a large, square chamber, papered in a flower design. The furniture was old and ugly. Two windows looked south, two east. All were prevented from opening more than six inches, top or bottom, by strong brass check chains, and the east windows, down which rain was pouring, were closed and locked.

"You're sure," Hoff asked Dace uncertainly, "you're *sure* no one came in through the door?"

"Positive," Oliver told him.

Chief Hoff had lost his ruddy color. He wiped his brow.

"But—the windows?" he suggested, almost appealingly.

Oliver shook his head.

"Obviously impossible!"

"Gosh!" the chief muttered, dabbing at his brow again.

"I think it safe to say no one could have entered the room in any possible manner between the time Nurse Minor left it and the time she returned," Kohn remarked calmly.

"No one human!"

It was Nurse Minor who gasped out the exclamation. Dr. Clane wheeled on her sharply.

"Now, Miss Minor!" he warned. "Don't let yourself get jumpy."

"But——" the nurse wailed. "But—if no one——"

"That will do, Miss Minor!" the doctor said authoritatively, and the woman was silent.

Madame Fage looked very shriveled and ancient in the glare of the lights. The knife had penetrated through her nightdress and into her chest. A stain of crimson surrounded it.

"That is the knife you gave Madame Fage?" Oliver asked of Kohn.

"It is. She wanted it, I imagined, because it is valuable."

"She kept it on this stand beside her bed," Nurse Minor said faintly. "Once she—she waved it at me because I wasn't fast enough."

Chief Hoff started around the room suddenly, rapping on the walls and stamping on the floor. He completed the circuit of the room and returned.

"I was lookin' for secret panels, or a trap door," he told them stubbornly.

"I have never heard of any in this house," Kohn said with amusement.

Chief Hoff turned to Oliver Dace.

"Look," he said, " I ain't joking. Could she 'a' been killed by something that shoots daggers through the window, or out of a panel in the wall, like I read about in books?"

Professor Natzof Kohn smiled.

"My dear Chief," he said, "books and life are entirely different matters. If such a thing were possible, there would be some evidence of it. There is none."

The chief gazed at the unbroken paper of the walls, the unmarred plaster of the ceiling, and looked flustered.

"Then she committed suicide!" he blurted out.

Dr. Clane shot a perplexed glance at Oliver.

"It is possible," he admitted reluctantly. "The knife was heavy. She could have driven it into her heart without difficulty. And then, in her dying struggles, have fallen from the bed."

"I think it should be obvious that is the answer," Kohn said, shrugging. "The knife unfortunately handy, her nerves on edge, an hysterical impulse—and there you are."

"Perhaps so," Oliver Dace replied. "I find it hard to believe."

Kohn smiled.

"If she was alone, and she did not commit suicide, you have the absurd alternative that she was not killed by human hands."

Oliver started to reply, but before he could speak Nurse Minor covered her mouth with a handkerchief and promptly fainted.

After the nurse had been lifted to a chair and revived, Chief Hoff, without looking at Professor Kohn, said loudly:

"I say she committed suicide!"

Still not looking at the tall, pale man, the chief addressed him.

"Kohn," he said, "how much you had to do with this I don't know. Maybe what you said this evening had something to do with it, maybe not. Maybe you scared her into killing herself. Or maybe—but never mind that. Anyway, she committed suicide. That's going to be my report. And now I'm leaving. And I ain't coming back."

Professor Kohn bowed.

"I assure you that I am desolate over this occurrence," he said unctuously, opening the door for the heavy man. Chief Hoff strode through it. Kohn gave the others an enigmatic glance and followed him.

"I am immeasurably shaken by this tragic occurrence, my friends——" they heard him saying.

Oliver Dace closed the door.

"Now," he said sternly, "we may search for the truth. Nurse Minor, do you feel strong enough to do something for me?"

"I-I'll try," the nurse said quaveringly.

"Can you go into the living room and fetch me the other knife, and do it so Kohn won't notice you?"

Nurse Minor quivered.

"Do—do I have to?" she asked. "I'm so afraid of knives."

"It is necessary."

"All right," Nurse Minor said unhappily, and went out.

"Oliver," Dr. Clane demanded as the nurse left, "what do you really think?"

Oliver Dace shook his head briefly, frowning.

"I confess I am puzzled," he said. "Only this I am sure of— Madame Fage did not kill herself."

"Oliver!" the doctor protested. "Surely, you don't think that——"

"Albert," his friend asked, "don't you believe Kohn was responsible for this death?"

"Well," the doctor admitted, "yes. I am sure he planned it. But by indirection. Psychological suggestion. As for anything else—well, of course the thought is nonsense."

"Maybe," Oliver answered absently.

A timid knock sounded at the door. Oliver opened it. Nurse Minor, shivering, thrust at him the second knife."

"T-take it," she chattered. "I'm af-f-fraid."

Oliver took the heavy blade from her.

"Thank you, Miss Minor. Now you had better go to your room. I'll take you back to town with me presently."

"Th-thank you," she got out, and turned, ran down the hall.

"She might well be frightened," Oliver commented. "So are all those people out there frightened—frightened through and through. This very minute they're whispering of black magic among themselves, and half believing it. Kohn did his work well."

He sat down on the edge of the narrow bed and, leaning over, held the second dagger close to the one driven into the old woman's breast.

"Identical," he remarked.

There was a noise of feet in the hall. Dr. Clane peered out.

"They're leaving," he said. "Like stampeded cattle."

"I don't blame them," Oliver Dace replied.

He held the point of the knife in his hand close to the blade of its twin.

"No question but that these would sink into one easily," he muttered. "They're as sharp as scalpels. Well!"

He had let the point of the knife touch the other blade. For an instant as he pulled it away it clung there with a soft but definite persistence. Oliver Dace placed the two steel blades together again. Almost like living creatures they clung together.

"Well!" Oliver Dace exclaimed again.

"There is something about those knives," the doctor said. "As if there really was something—something living in them."

"Perhaps," Oliver agreed abstractedly. "Perhaps there is."

Dr. Clane watched with bewilderment as he took out a pocketknife and opened a blade. Gently he rubbed the blade of the knife against the steel of the dagger he held. Then he rubbed the knife against the exposed portion of the blade that had killed Madame Fage.

"Curious!" he said to himself.

Dr. Clane took a nervous stride or two.

"Oliver," he said, "I don't blame those folks for running. I almost feel like bolting myself. Though I know that—possibly through Kohn's suggestion, it is true—Madame Fage killed herself, yet I feel . . . Well, blast it, I feel almost as if magic really had been done here tonight. Black magic."

Oliver Dace glanced at him, his eyes half shrouded in thought.

"There are more powers in the world than we imagine," he said slowly. "But," he added, "putting aside the mysteries that are beyond us, there is still magic which I can understand.

And it is my belief that through the use of magic Professor Kohn killed Madame Fage."

Dr. Clane made a despairing gesture.

"Oliver," he said, "don't ask me to believe that. I can't."

Oliver Dace was balancing the heavy knife in his hand when it slipped from his grasp. The weapon fell to the floor, the point biting deeply into the wood beside Oliver's foot. It stood upright, quivering faintly. Oliver plucked it free.

"Professor Kohn has gone outside to speed the departing townsfolk," he remarked. "Go and make sure he is still there. Detain him for ten minutes—fifteen if you can. I will need at least ten minutes to myself."

Dr. Clane gazed at him in bafflement before he turned.

"Very well," he agreed, and went out.

He was gone for fifteen minutes. When he returned, it was to find the room dimmed. Only a small table lamp was burning. The body of Madame Fage had been straightened and laid upon the bed, and in the dim light the face was as brown and shriveled as an ancient mummy's. Oliver Dace was wiping his hands on a handkerchief, and breathing a bit fast.

"Where is Kohn?" he asked.

"Outside, on the porch," the doctor told him. "He won't stay there much longer, though. Too wet. I drew him aside with Chief Hoff and kept their attention with talk about coroners. The chief was anxious to go; the professor quite willing to discuss details. Oliver, the man is laughing at us all!"

"Perhaps," Oliver suggested, "we can silence his amusement."

"Oliver," Dr. Clane demanded, "what have you done with

the knife?"

"I am working great magic with it," Oliver Dace told him earnestly. "Albert, help me move Madame Fage's bed out from the wall."

Clane assisted his friend to slide the narrow bed away from the papered wall, until a space three feet wide was left.

"Do you suspect a trap door here?" he asked.

"No, I think we can be sure there are no secret entrances to this room."

"Then I do not understand what you are doing," Dr. Clane said in bewilderment.

"Do you remember what Professor Kohn did just before the nurse screamed?"

Dr. Clane thought a moment.

"He turned on the lights," he replied finally.

Oliver nodded. "Why did he do that?"

"Why—to get more light."

"He was working magic," Oliver Dace told him. "Did you ever stop to think that turning on a light from a point far distant from it is a type of magic for which our forefathers would have burned you?"

"Why no," the doctor confessed. "I never thought of it that way."

"Yet it is magic," Oliver insisted. "The magic of science."

"I am afraid I still do not follow you."

His friend's face was stern. "All evening," he said, "Professor Natzof Kohn stood out in that room, controlling the forces of evil, and laughing to himself. The man is brilliant, diabolically brilliant.

"He has raised murder to the height of a dramatic art. As you say, he knew he would be the first to be suspected if anything happened to Madame Fage. So the audience here tonight was invited for just one purpose—to witness his complete innocence, yet never to know for sure he was not guilty. Never to know for sure that he had not, perhaps, worked before their very eyes the black magic he was telling them about.

"Doctor, step out into the other room and——"

"And do what?" The voice of Professor Natzof Kohn cut off his words like a whiplash.

Unnoticed, he had come to the door of the room. For a moment he stood there staring at Oliver Dace, his triangular face shining with a pale light from the overhead lamp. Then he stepped into the room. His eyes shot to the bed that Oliver and Dr. Clane had moved out from the wall.

"What have you been doing?" Kohn demanded. "Why did you move that bed?"

He took one swift step and was beside the bed. That he might still face them, he stepped into the narrow space between it and the wall.

"Have you been searching the knife, perhaps, for fingerprints?" he sneered. "I assure you there are none. The power which that knife obeys does not leave fingerprints."

Oliver Dace eyed him steadily.

"Yet it left its mark upon the knife," he said quietly, "for any man to read. And I have read it. And I know how you killed

Madame Fage."

The tall man leaned swiftly over the dead woman, his long body bent like a bow.

"You lie!" he said. "The powers which I control——"

His next word was never spoken. There was a single instant when terrific light flooded the room and then a crash of thunder that seemed to shake the walls stunned them. The light in the room flickered, then went out. For a space of three heartbeats the room was in darkness, and in the darkness, as the thunder died away, Oliver Dace and Dr. Clane heard a queer thudding sound followed by a little scuffle, as if a man had fallen a short distance. Then silence.

When the lights came up again, they saw that Natzof Kohn had fallen forward across the bed where his dead benefactress lay. And standing out from his bent back was the wooden handle of the second knife.

Chief of Police Hoff, overtaken and brought back, and Dr. Clane stared in silence into the space where Oliver Dace had ripped up the floor in the second-story bedroom that had been Natzof Kohn's. Nestled between the supporting beams was an apparatus of many coils of wire about a steel core.

"There," Oliver Dace said, "is magic. Scientific magic. That is an electromagnet. Natzof Kohn made and installed it for the sole purpose of committing murder."

They followed him downstairs. In the bedroom of Madame Fage, Oliver pointed at the ceiling, directly above the normal position of the bed.

"Up there," he said, "the electromagnet lies just a fraction of an inch above the plaster. Kohn no doubt managed to install it last month when, you tell me, some repair work was done to the house. Connected through a switch in the living room, he was able to turn it on or off from there.

"This evening Natzof Kohn entered this room. Having turned on the electromagnet, he reached the ceiling by means of a stepladder I found down the hall, and placed the knife against it. The hard steel of the blade clung with a firm grip to the invisible bonds of magnetic attraction, held against the ceiling without visible support.

"Madame Fage, having weak eyes, used only dim lights. In the dimness the knife would not be noticed. Madame Fage slept upon her back, as many people do, and the deadly blade was over her heart. Natzof Kohn, as soon as he knew she was in bed and alone in the room, turned that switch in the living room, and shut off the electromagnet.

"At once the great blade fell from the ceiling. You saw, Doctor, how the blade plunged into the floor upright when I dropped it? In just that way did it drive itself into the heart of Madame Fage."

After a silence, Chief Hoff spoke.

"But," he asked, "what about Kohn?"

Oliver Dace shook his head.

"I knew how Kohn had killed Madame Fage. But I wished to test the apparatus without his knowledge before accusing him. I went into the living room while Dr. Clane engaged Kohn's attention and turned the light switch that controlled the electromagnet. Then I got the ladder, placed the second knife against the ceiling, where the magnetism held it, and replaced the ladder.

"A moment later Kohn entered the room. He saw that I had moved the bed, was alarmed, and to see what I had been doing, he stepped into the narrow space between the bed and the wall. I had intended for the knife to plunge into the floor when I shut off the electromagnet.

"But in that instant, as Kohn stood there, lightning struck somewhere near the house. Perhaps it struck the power lines, for the electricity failed for several seconds. When it failed, the electromagnet ceased to work, releasing the second knife. It plunged downward, straight into Kohn's back."

"And killed him," Chief Hoff said.

"And killed him," Oliver agreed. "I first began to understand when I accidentally touched the first blade to the second. They clung together. Magnetism. I tested both with my penknife. The blade that had killed Madame Fage was magnetized. The other was not. Hard steel placed in a field of magnetic force becomes magnetized. Then I suspected."

They were silent until presently Oliver spoke again.

"The magic of science, misused to an evil purpose, killed Madame Fage," he said. "The same force struck down her murderer. That we know. But what we cannot know is what higher force induced Natzof Kohn to step into that small space and bow his back just at the instant a stroke of lightning made the power fail, so that he might receive death from his own contrivance."

The Glass Bridge

We were discussing unsolved murders, the Baron de Hirsch,
Lieutenant Oliver Baynes of the State Police, and I. At least,
de Hirsch was discussing them. Baynes and I were allowed
only to listen while the tall, hawk-nosed Hungarian, with scin-
tillating deduction and logic, solved half a dozen famous cases
which remain in the files of various police departments still
marked "Open."

De Hirsch can be a very irritating companion. His self-
assurance is colossal, and his appreciation of his own cleverness

is unconcealed. I am always tempted to ask him why, if he's so smart, his shoes always need repairing and his clothes mending. But I never do.

I could see Oliver Baynes getting restless. Baynes is short and dumpy, red-faced, slow-spoken and unimpressive. But he's a good cop—one of the best.

He mopped his brow—it was a hot August afternoon—and looked across at me. We were sitting in the living room of my summer cottage in the Berkshires.

"Get your friend to solve the case of the blonde blackmailer for us," he said, the sarcasm in the remark hidden behind a completely blank expression.

De Hirsch paused. His deep-set eyes glinted; his large, beaked nose flared.

"The case of the blonde blackmailer?" he asked, softly, politely.

"Her name was Marianne Montrose." Baynes said. "Last February 13th, between three and four in the afternoon, she walked up twenty-three snow covered steps to a house on a hilltop about thirty miles from here. She went into that house and never came out again.

"Later we searched the house and she wasn't there. There was snow two feet deep all around the house. There wasn't a mark in it to show she had been taken away in any manner. Besides, the owner and only resident is a man with a heart condition who could be killed by any exertion. So he didn't carry her away or dig a hole and bury her or anything like that. But she wasn't there, and she was seen to enter, and her footsteps went up in the snow on the steps. Went up and never came down again. You tell us what happened to her."

De Hirsch's eyes held steady on Baynes.

"Give me the facts," he said, "and I will."

He didn't say he'd try, he said he would.

"I'll get my fact sheets," I told him, nettled. "It'll be nice to know the truth. Besides, I'll get another article out of it."

I went to my files and brought back the folder on Marianne Montrose. It was pretty complete. As a true-crime writer for the popular magazines, I keep detailed notes on every case I use. I had already written this one up, giving it the Big Question Mark or "What Mappened to Lovely Marianne?" treatment.

"Where do you want to start?" I asked. "Here's the statement of young Danny Gresham, the last person who spoke to Marianne before she went into the house and vanished."

De Hirsch waved away the typescript.

"Read it to me," he said, his manner gracious.

Oliver Baynes made a noise through his nose. He might have been laughing. I glared at him and began to read:

*   *   *

Morgan's Gap, Feb. 3. From statement by Daniel Gresham, age 19.

I was in the office of the *Morgan's Gap Weekly Sentinel*, reading proof. It was half-past three. The temperature outside was about eight above zero, I guess, maybe six. It was a nice brisk day. I was thinking of calling up my girl, Dolly Hansome, and making a date to go skiing. The snow was nice and deep, with a good crust on it, and some fresh snow on top. While I was thinking about Dolly, a snappy blue hardtop pulled to a stop outside.

There was a girl driving. She looked like Dolly Hansome, but taller and better developed—more womanly, that is. She had blonde hair, long and curly under a red cap, and was wearing a red ski suit. She got out and stood looking across the valley and up the slope toward Mr. Mark Hillyer the mystery writer's house. The Eyrie, Mr. Hillyer calls it. That means nest. It's a very good name for it, the way it perches all by itself on top of the ridge.

You might think it was a funny place for a man with a bad heart to live all by himself. In the summer you can drive right around and up to the back of the house where the terrace is, but in the winter the town only cleans the road up to the steps out in front.

That means that Mr. Hillyer never leaves the house after the first big snow, but he doesn't seem to care. In the fall he puts in three thousand gallons of fuel oil and a big stock of canned goods and he's all set. Every day Mrs. Hoff goes up to cook and clean. She doesn't mind the steps and neither does her brother-in-law, Sam. He keeps the steps swept, and clears off the north terrace.

Mr. Hillyer likes to be alone. He doesn't care for people. He's a tall, thin man with a long, disappointed face and a sharp way of saying things. He's written twelve mystery books and has a lot of clippings and reviews. He's especially proud of the ones that mention how clever his plots are. He hasn't written any new books for five years, though. I guess he's discouraged because the ones he did before never sold very well.

Oh, sure, about the girl.

She stood looking up at the house, then turned and came in the office. I jumped up to help her. She smiled and said hello. Her voice was low and husky and sort of gave you a tingly feeling, if you know what I mean. She asked if I was the editor. I said I was the assistant. Then she asked if she could use the phone. I said sure, of course, certainly, and handed it to her. She asked for Mark Hillyer's number. I couldn't help hearing what she said. Sure I remember the words, just about.

"Hello, Mark," she said, and her voice was different now. "This is Marianne. I'm phoning from the village. I trust you're expecting me and, Mark, darling—just in case you might have been getting any funny ideas in that clever brain of yours— they know here at the newspaper office I'm coming up to see you. I'll be up in ten minutes."

She hung up and smiled at me, and her voice was back again the way it had been.

"Mark Hillyer doesn't like me," she said. "And he's a very clever man. I do think he would kill me if he could get away with it. But he can't. Just the same, if I'm not back here in an hour, you'll send the police up to look for me, won't you? I'll stop on my way back, just to let you know I'm all right."

She smiled at me again and naturally I said sure, of course, I'd get Constable Redman to come up and look for her. I was pretty thrilled; it was sort of like a scene out of one of Mr.

Hillyer's books. Of course, I didn't think she really meant what she'd said. But when she drove off, I went to the window to watch her.

She drove away, and a minute later I saw her car starting up the road that winds around to get to Mr. Hillyer's Eyrie. A lot of kids were out on the lower slope with skis and sleds and these new aluminum bowls having a swell time sliding all over the place.

I saw the convertible reach the turnaround at the foot of the steps to Hillyer's house—the snowplows clear it out. The girl parked the car and got out. She started up that flight of steps. I saw her reach Mr. Hillyer's little front porch. The door opened. She went in and the door closed.

I kept an eye on Mr. Hillyer's house all the rest of the afternoon as I worked, until it got dark. But the girl never came out again.

End of statement by Daniel Gresham.

    ✻   ✻   ✻

I paused and glanced at de Hirsch. He sat back, his head cradled on the back of the chair, staring upward at my ceiling.

"A most interesting opening for a murder case," he said tolerantly, looking at me. "Naturally, any theory I have at this point must be completely tentative. Please continue."

I read:

    ✻   ✻   ✻

Morgan's Gap, Feb. 14. From statement by Constable Harvey Redman.

At about five-thirty yesterday young Danny Gresham came busting into my office, saying a pretty girl had gone up to see Mr. Mark Hillyer and might be in danger. At first I thought it was more of his imagination, but he gave me all the facts and I figured maybe we'd better go see. Anybody who writes books like Hillyer does might just as easy kill someone for real.

I got flashlights and we went in my old car. We got to Hillyer's place just about six. Sure enough, there was Miss Montrose's convertible still parked in the turn-around. And Danny showed me a woman's prints in the drifted snow on the steps.

There was one set of prints going up.

None coming down.

So he was right about her still being there, anyway.

We climbed up, stepping wide of the prints, and knocked. Mr. Hillyer let us in, looking surprised. I told him what the woman had told Danny, and asked where Miss Montrose was. Mr. Hillyer laughed.

"I'm afraid Miss Montrose is having a joke on you and Danny," he said. "She left here an hour ago, just about dark."

"Mr. Hillyer," I told him, "there's a woman's footprints coming up your steps and none going down. Besides, her car is still there."

"By George, that's odd!" Mr. Hillyer said, but he said it as if he were laughing.

"That's what I think," I told him. "That's why I'm asking where the lady is."

"But I don't know where she is," he said, looking me in the eye. "Constable, I'll be frank with you. That girl is a blackmailer. She came here today to collect a thousand dollars from me. I paid it. Then she left. And that's absolutely all I know. I insist that you search this house to see if you find any trace of her or evidence that I did anything to her. All I want is to be in the clear."

Danny and I searched the house. Mr. Hillyer sat in his chair by the fireplace in his writing den, smoking and waiting.

The house was easy to search, being only six rooms on one floor. No cellar, no attic. Oil burner's in a little closet. Floors are cement. Walls are double cinder block with insulation in between.

The girl wasn't in the house. No trace she'd ever been there, either. No signs of a struggle, no bloodstains.

Danny and I went outside. There weren't any marks in the snow around the house. The north terrace had been shoveled off, but the snow had drifted right up to it and there was a light sprinkle of snow on the tiles. No marks in it at all. That didn't mean an awful lot, though, because the drifts went all the way down the slope to Harrison's Gully, a quarter mile away almost. There's usually a breeze coming up from the gully and it would lay more snow on the terrace pretty quick.

Danny tried the crust, though, and broke right through, after only a step. Nobody could have gone over that snow without leaving marks. Besides, Mr. Hillyer's heart would have killed him if he'd tried.

So, after we looked in the garage and searched the car and

especially the trunk without finding her, we told Mr. Hillyer it looked like Miss Montrose had left all right.

"I'm glad you're satisfied I'm not hiding her, Constable." He chuckled. "In spite of the story she gave Danny, and in spite of her footprints coming only toward the house and her car still being there, it's perfectly obvious I couldn't have killed her and hidden her body—unless of course I carried it away over a glass bridge."

I told him I didn't follow that.

"Why, Constable," he said, "I guess you don't know your mystery fiction. One of the most famous stories is about a man who's killed by a glass knife. Then the murderer drops the weapon in a pitcher of water and it becomes invisible and nobody can find it. So maybe I killed Miss Montrose and carried her away over a glass bridge—one that's invisible now. Or I have another theory for you. Maybe a flying saucer came down and whisked her away. In fact, the more I think about it the more I imagine that's what must have happened."

"I don't guess you're taking this very serious, Mr. Hillyer," I told him. "But I am and I'm going to call in the State Police."

So I did. Let them decide where that girl went. I got other things to bother about right now.

End of statement by Constable Harvey Redman.

＊　　＊　　＊

I stopped reading. De Hirsch opened his eyes.

"Admirably complete," he said kindly. "You're a good researcher even if you haven't much imagination." He turned to Baynes. "I suppose you took over the case then, Lieutenant?"

"Yeah," Baynes grunted, eyeing him. "But not until Troopers Reynolds and Rivkin had answered the constable's call. They made a search. Same results. Then the case got dumped in my lap. I get all the screwy cases. I went out the next day. But questioning Hillyer was like asking the cat what happened to the canary. He talked about the blackmail angle, though. Said he'd made a slip years ago, and Montrose knew about it. Since then he'd been paying her off a thousand dollars a year. Every year, when she happened to be near, she'd let him know she was coming over in a day or two and he'd get the thousand ready in cash for her.

"I checked with New York. She was in the racket, all right. So his story was probably true. I checked the local bank, too. They'd mailed him ten hundreds just three days before.

"I looked around the house. Just like the constable and my troopers said. Crusty snow but not strong enough to hold up a man. Even skis left marks. Maybe a toboggan wouldn't have.

"Trouble was, he'd never had anything like a toboggan, or even skiis or a sled, in the house. Mrs. Hoff had cleaned that morning and even gone into the garage to get her cleaning things. She'd have seen anything as big as a toboggan, and she swore the whole idea was just a pipe dream. And he couldn't have ordered one special by phone because it would have had to be delivered and nobody had delivered anything but food or mail there for weeks. I checked.

"I didn't have any other theory to take its place, though. The girl had to go somewhere! I got four troopers who could ski, and set them to covering all the region around the house. They covered everything within a quarter of a mile, including a couple of small dips and gullies, and didn't find a trace of her or of any track in the snow. Then it started snowing again and I had to call the search off. But I'd made sure she wasn't any place where she could be found.

"Hillyer enjoyed every minute of it. He enjoyed giving interviews and he posed for pictures. He passed out autographed copies of his books to the feature writers. He looked ten years younger all of a sudden; he was having so much fun.

"He passed out plenty of double talk about the mystery of it all. He quoted this guy Charles Fort, who wrote about mysterious disappearances. He talked about spontaneous vanishment, and warps in the space-time continuum, and abduction by little green men in flying saucers. He had the time of his life.

"So, finally, we had to table the case. Absolutely all we really knew was what we knew to begin with. A girl walked up those steps into his house and just vanished. So we sat back to wait for new developments. Then came June."

Oliver Baynes paused to mop his face again.

De Hirsch nodded his great Roman head. "And in June," he said, "the body was found."

Baynes looked at him in surprise.

"Yes," he agreed. "In June, Marianne Montrose stopped being one kind of mystery and became another kind of mystery. You see——"

But de Hirsch had raised a restraining hand.

"Let Bob read it," he suggested. "I know he has it written out in a fine, dramatic style. And sometimes I find a certain pleasure in his prose."

So I read:

❖   ❖   ❖

Morgan's Gap, June 3. Based upon statements by Willy Johnson, age 11, and Ferdie Pulver, age 10.

The two boys stopped beside the deeply blue pool no more than thirty yards across. They were in a long, narrow depression with almost sheer sides fifty feet high. It ran for three hundred yards to a rocky ledge where a small waterfall emptied into the natural trap and flowed down to make the pool at their feet. The pool in turn emptied out through a narrow throat in the rock, just wide enough for a small boy to negotiate, too narrow to admit an adult.

Willows and alders, green with new leaves, stretched upward toward the sunlight. Redwing blackbirds darted in and out, and high overhead crows soared on black pinions. A chipmunk, unafraid, chattered at the boys from a branch.

They were barefoot, their shoes in their hands, and the water was icy cold. But, entranced by the secret little world of the gully, they hardly noticed the water's temperature.

"Gee!" Ferdie said. "This is swell. Let's bring a gang and play pirates, huh?"

"Pirates!" Willy sniffed. "Fishin' is more fun. C'mon, throw in your hook."

He thrust a reluctant worm onto the hook of a handline and tossed it into the pool. It rippled in the green water and sank from sight. He waited all of thirty seconds, then impatiently jerked it.

"Gosh!" he shouted. "I caught something . . . aw, heck, it's snagged."

He pulled hard. The line came in, slowly, with an almost unyielding dead weight. Ferdie wasn't paying any attention. He was staring up the gully to where a small fragment of something white dangled from a silver-green willow.

"What's that?" he asked nervously. "You thinking it's a ghost, huh, Willy?"

"Heck, no." Willy didn't even look. He was gasping as he tugged in his line. "Gee, I got a big branch or somethin'."

Something dark and red surged upward to the surface, and broke the water with a slow swirling motion. Then the awkward mass turned over and a pale, oval face appeared, surrounded by a halo of golden hair that rippled in the water with a life of its own.

"Hey!" Willy shrilled. "It's a deader! C'mon, Ferdie, let's get out of here!"

Behind them, as their yells died out in the distance, the pale face and golden hair seemed to hesitate for a moment, as if waiting. Then they sank slowly back into the dark, quiet depths from which they had come. . . .

❊   ❊   ❊

"Well," Oliver Baynes took up the narration, "Willy's parents called the constable and the constable called me. A couple of hours later half a dozen of us got out up at Mark Hillyer's house. The only decent way to reach the gully without doing mountain climbing was to go down through Hillyer's property. He was perfectly agreeable, and when we told him what we were up to he seemed only mildly interested.

" 'If you find her,' he said, 'look in the pocket of her ski suit. She had a thousand dollars of mine when she left and I shall put in a claim for it.'

"We reached the gully, over some very rough ground, and lowered in on ropes. Then we started grappling for the body. We found it inside of twenty minutes. As it came up, Danny Gresham—who was with us—gave a yell.

" 'That's her! But how'd she get here so far from the house? She must have flown!'

"She looked well preserved—that water was almost ice cold. She had ten hundred-dollar bills in her ski suit pocket, too. We grappled some more, and finally came up with her ski cap and one mitten. I left the men grappling, and made a search of the gully myself. Outside of a few old beer bottles and some tin cans, there wasn't a thing that shouldn't have been there.

"We grappled in that pool all day. I was still hoping to find a toboggan or something, but we never did. Nothing. There was the body, a quarter mile from the house, and no clues as to how it got there.

"We lifted the body out and had an autopsy. She'd died of cold and exposure. Stomach was empty—no telling how long after her last meal she'd died. No trace of poison in tissues."

Oliver Baynes looked challengingly at de Hirsch.

"Well," he said, "there's your case of the blonde blackmailer. Now let's hear you explain it without any double-talk about spontaneous vanishment, warps in the space-time continuum, glass bridges and flying saucers."

"I can't," my friend said blandly. And as a look of guarded triumph appeared on Baynes' red features, de Hirsch added, "Without mentioning the glass bridge, the flying saucer, and above all the winding sheet."

"Oh, sure!" Lieutenant Baynes looked disgusted. "Give us some more jabberwocky and admit you don't know what happened to that girl!"

"But I can't do that," de Hirsch objected, giving Baynes a pleasant look. "Because, you see, I know what happened to her. At least, I will know when you add the one item you have left out of your narration."

"Left out?" Baynes blinked.

"The white object Ferdie Pulver thought might be a ghost," de Hirsch said.

"Oh that!" Baynes shrugged. "That was just an old, tattered bedsheet, tangled in the branches of the willow trees. Had Hillyer's laundry mark. He said it must have blown off the clothesline during a windy spell in the spring. It didn't mean a thing. We had experts go over it, practically thread by thread. Just an old bedsheet."

"Not a bedsheet," de Hirsch murmured in gentle correction. "A winding sheet. Thus it is as I said—a glass bridge, a flying saucer and a winding sheet. Don't you see, in the arrogance of his pride in his own intellect, Hillyer told you the truth! He gave you all the clues. At least, he gave them to Constable Redman and they were in the constable's statement. He killed Marianne Montrose, and whisked her away in a flying saucer over a glass bridge to nowhere—which is to say, eternity."

Baynes chewed his under lip. He stared at de Hirsch, puzzled. So did I. It was exactly the situation de Hirsch enjoyed most—when he could dispense bafflement in the guise of enlightenment.

Slowly Baynes reached into his pocket. He took out a wallet. From the wallet he took a twenty dollar bill.

"Twenty dollars say you're just double-talking, like Hillyer," he stated flatly.

De Hirsch's eyes brightened. Then he sighed and shook his head.

"No," he murmured. "We are both guests of an old and valued friend. It would not be the act of a gentleman to take money from another guest on such a simple matter."

Now Baynes gritted his teeth. He took two more bills from his wallet.

"Fifty dollars say you don't know any more than we do," he snapped.

De Hirsch turned deep, black eyes on me. I hastily computed what I would receive for a true detective article I'd recently finished, and took out my checkbook.

"I'll say a hundred you can't give us the solution," I announced, looking him fixedly in the eye. I knew my Hungarian friend did not have a hundred, did not have fifty, and I doubted if he had five.

The Baron de Hirsch straightened. "You make it impossible for me, as a gentleman, to refuse," he said. "But I'll need some help . . . I'll need a clothespin."

Baynes' open mouth closed. My closed mouth opened.

"In the left-hand drawer beside the kitchen sink," I said. "Should be some there. Mrs. Ruggles, the cleaning woman . . ."

Rising with a single lithe motion, de Hirsch had already left the room, taking out a large, immaculate linen handkerchief as he went. And a fountain pen.

I looked at Baynes. He looked at me. Neither of us spoke. De Hirsch was gone about five minutes. I heard a drawer open. I heard a muffled sound that might have been the icebox opening, or the deep freeze. Presently he came back and sat down.

"It will take a few minutes," he said. "Meanwhile, we can talk. What do you think of the political situation?"

"Never mind the political situation," Baynes growled. "What about Hillyer and the girl? How did he kill her?"

De Hirsch struck his palm against his head.

"I forgot to ask!" he exclaimed. "Does Hillyer suffer from insomnia?"

Baynes wrinkled his brows. "Yeah," he said. "He does. That was part of the report I got from his doc. But what——"

"Naturally, I assumed it," de Hirsch broke in. "But of course, one must never assume anything. Why, Lieutenant, Hillyer killed her by putting sleeping tablets in a drink. When she was unconscious, he whisked her away and buried her in the deep snow of Harrison's Gully. There, in due time, her body absorbed the sleeping potion. She awoke, nearly frozen. For a brief, a mercifully brief time she struggled against the iron bonds that held her. Then the soft sleep that comes to those who freeze took her and in gentle arms carried her down the long dark steps that led to death."

"Very fancy prose," Baynes grunted. "But you haven't said anything. There weren't any bonds of any kind. Not a mark on her. Nothing. Maybe he did knock her out with sleeping tablets. That I figured. But then what?"

The Baron de Hirsch took his time about answering.

"Tell me, Bob—" he turned to me—"would you say Mark Hillyer has achieved a minor form of immortality from this case? The fame that he always sought, and never found?"

"He certainly has," I agreed. "Already there's a big argument among crime fans as to whether he did or didn't kill her. The mystery of how she got into the gully is as tantalizing as the mystery of what happened to the famous Dorothy Arnold. A hundred years from now, Hillyer's name should still be popping up in books as the double-domes of the next century argue about his guilt or innocence. As Baynes said, he's riding high. He has a new book due out, and all his old ones have been reprinted. He's famous, all right, and he'll stay famous as long as the case goes unsolved. In fact, the longer it goes unsolved, the more famous he'll be. Like Jack the Ripper."

"Ah," de Hirsch said. "And as soon as it is solved, he is merely infamous—a sordid murderer. A shock to an ego— especially to one such as his. But now I think we can discuss the mystery of the glass bridge, the flying saucer and the winding sheet—all of them invisible."

He rose and went to the kitchen. Again I heard the ice box, or the deep freeze, open and shut. He came back carrying something balanced on his hand. It was covered with a napkin so we could not see what it was. He set the object on the polished top of the coffee table.

"Now," he said, his voice suddenly crisp and authoritative, "let us go back to last February. It is a bitterly cold afternoon. Mark Hillyer, bleakly furious, stands at the window, waiting to see a blackmailer's car drive up. We know what else he saw— children at play. Watching them, an idea exploded in his mind, complete and exquisite, like Minerva springing from Jove's forehead. He could be rid of his blackmailer quite safely, needing only a minimum of luck. If he failed—well, he was a sick man and could plead provocation. If he succeeded—what a pleasure to watch the stupid world puzzle over the mystery he had created!

"He acted at once. He got an old bedsheet, the largest he owned, and spread it flat on the flagstones of the north terrace. He did certain things to it, and went back inside. A few minutes later Miss Montrose arrived. He talked with her, gave her a drink heavy with sleeping potion. In twenty minutes or so she collapsed, unconscious.

"He tumbled her from her chair to the floor. He nudged her onto a small rug which could be easily pulled. No exertion, you see, nothing to strain his bad heart.

"He slid the rug across the floor and out onto the north

terrace. There he rolled the unconscious woman onto the spread-out bedsheet. He arranged her so that she was curled up in the center of it. . . ."

With a theatrical gesture, de Hirsch whipped the napkin off the object on the table. We saw that it was his linen handkerchief. Something lay in the center of the handkerchief—a clothespin, with little eyes and a mouth inked on it, as if it were a woman reduced to scale, and the handkerchief a bedsheet.

To see the clothespin doll, I had to pry up one corner of the handkerchief. For each of the four corners had been folded into the center, completely covering the thing, as if in an envelope. And the handkerchief was stiff and hard.

Then we saw what de Hirsch had done. He had sprinkled water on the handkerchief and put it into the deep freeze. Like laundry on a wash line on a winter day, the handkerchief had become stiff, unbending. Inside it, imprisoned in it, was the clothespin representing a woman. The whole thing made a neat package several inches square. If it had been a real bedsheet and a real woman curled up in the center of it, it would have been no more than three feet square.

And now at last Baynes and I began to understand all that Mark Hillyer had done. He had sprinkled a large bedsheet with water on a bitterly cold day. He had put an unconscious woman in the center of it, curled up, and then folded the corners over her. The cold had frozen the wet bedsheet into a sort of box as stiff and hard as board. In a matter of minutes Marianne Montrose, unconscious, was a prisoner inside a frozen shroud that was as formidable as iron bonds.

Then Hillyer had thrust the broad, flat object off the terrace onto the hard-surfaced snow. Because of the dispersal of weight, it had left no mark on the crust. Instead it had slipped away smoothly down the slope, picking up speed, whisking over rough spots, until at last it shot off the edge of the crusty snow and tumbled deep into the clinging drifts of wind-blown snow within the permanently shadowed depths of the gully.

As if in example, de Hirsch flicked the frozen handkerchief with his finger. It spun across the table and off the edge, dropping into a wastebasket. There, among white sheets of discarded typewriter paper, it suddenly vanished.

"A flying saucer," de Hirsch boomed. "In Danny Gresham's statement, he specifically mentioned the new aluminum bowls some of the children were playing with in the snow. These are metal saucers in which a child sits and whisks down a slope at truly terrifying speed. They ride the surface, scarcely sinking into a crust at all. It was these that Hillyer saw, these from which he gained his idea.

"The glass bridge was already there—a slick, thin coating of ice which covered the drifts from his house to Harrison's Gully. The flying saucer he made from a sheet sprayed with water in the icy air. And it became the girl's winding sheet when he laid her upon it and folded the edges over her and froze them down.

"Off it went, spinning, sliding, skidding. It could not stop. Over the edge, into the gully. A white object in white snow.

Invisible to the searching eyes. A little wind-blown snow over it, and it had vanished. To find it one would have had to step on it. Little chance of that.

"*Lássd!* Or to put it in English, there you have it! A baffling, an impenetrable mystery has been created by the use of an old bedsheet and the natural forces of winter. A woman has been transported a quarter of a mile by means of a seemingly miraculous agency. A sick man has committed the seemingly perfect murder!"

"The rat!" Baynes burst out. "Telling me to my face how he did it, and making me think he was double-talking me! Why, that girl and that sheet probably hung in the branches of that tree until spring. Then when the thaw came, the sheet unfroze, she fell out and was carried along by the brook down into the pool, leaving nothing—no trace, no clue, just an old bedsheet!"

"But if one with imagination sees the bedsheet as a winding sheet—" de Hirsch reached for the money and my check, on the table—"and if one takes the remarks of a clever man at face value, a mystery may become quite commonplace."

"We'll never be able to prove it," Baynes growled.

"Perhaps not," de Hirsch commented. "But we can let him know that his mystery is a mystery no longer, and that he will be the subject of no so-clever studies of homicide in the year 2000. I will write him a letter."

He went off to my study and typed for half an hour. He mailed the letter that same afternoon. The next morning Mark Hillyer received it. I don't know what it said, but Oliver Baynes, via the housekeeper, described its reception.

Mrs. Hoff was dusting in the study when the mailman came. She took the letter to Hillyer on the terrace, and he interrupted his writing to open it. He had hardly more than glanced at it when he became deathly pale—so pale that Mrs. Hoff turned back in alarm. As he read further, an ugly, mottled flush spread over his features. He scarcely looked at the second page before ripping the letter up and flinging the pieces into a big ash tray. He lit a match with hands that shook so violently he could hardly bring the match head to the striking surface, and burned the torn pieces.

As if still unable to relieve his rage, he seized the ash tray and flung it furiously down on the tiles. For an instant, he stood looking north toward Harrison's Gully, his hands clenching and unclenching.

Then his breath began to come with difficulty. He turned, reaching for support, but collapsed before he could reach his chair. Clawing at his chest and throat, he gasped, "Medicine— my medicine . . ."

His heart stimulant was not in the medicine cabinet, but on his bedside table. It took Mrs. Hoff two or three minutes to find it. When she hurried back with it, Hillyer was dead.

I admit I was somehow shocked. But de Hirsch accepted Hillyer's death with composure.

"*Utovegre!*" he commented, in Hungarian. "Which is to say, it is as good as a confession."

Change of Address

"That house," Mrs. Hollins said positively—she was a positive woman—"is only fit for a murder."

Mr. Hollins, who was a small man with a merry twinkle in his eyes, chuckled.

"You've been reading too many books, Jocasta," he said. "It looks like quite a good house, really. Of course, it needs a few repairs. Otherwise it wouldn't be available these days, would it, Mr. Smiley?"

Mr. Smiley, the real estate agent from Port Oro, snapped his fingers.

"That's it, Mr. Hollins!" he said. "If that house was in tiptop shape it would have been rented long ago."

It could not be denied that the house, two stories with an exterior of stained shingles, needed repair. Green lichens stained the roof, and the front porch threatened collapse. Mrs. Hollins remarked as much.

"Details, my dear, details," Mr. Hollins said. "Look how cozily it nestles into the cliff! Notice how wide the beach in front of it is! See how those Pacific combers come rolling in, boom, boom, boom! Smell the ocean air!"

He drew in a deep breath.

"Fresh air, quiet, seclusion!" he said. "California climate! Why, I feel like a new man already."

Mrs. Hollins, who was tall and angular, sniffed.

"If by fresh air you mean the smell of dead fish, I agree," she stated. "As for the cliff, it will cut off the sunshine for all except a few hours a day. As for the ocean, I always thought the Pacific was blue, not grey. As for the beach——"

But little Mr. Hollins was moving briskly after the real estate agent.

"We'll see the inside before we make up our minds," he cried. "You say this place has a furnace, Mr. Smiley?"

Mr. Smiley showed them the furnace—sound, if rusty, due to a certain dampness that came from the earthen floor of the cellar.

"Not a house in twenty out here has a furnace," Mr. Smiley said impressively. "It's the great feature of this place. Any time a chilly snap comes along, you just light up and there you are, snug and warm. And if you want to get rid of the dampness, there's nothing to it. Just put in a cement floor, that's all."

"Of course!" Mr. Hollins said. "A cement floor. Exactly! It'll fix everything. Now let's see the upstairs, eh, my dear? Although I already know I like this house—like it very much."

Mr. Smiley, more optimistic, showed them the rest of the house.

"You see, pet?" remarked Mr. Hollins when they had finished. "Not bad, not bad at all. Rooms are a very nice size, kitchen is quite modern, the plumbing works, the floors don't squeak— some paint and polish and it'll be charming, really quite a little love nest." He even did a little dance step, such was his exuberance. "We'll take it, Mr. Smiley, we'll take it!"

"You might consult me on the matter," Mrs. Hollins said. "Since presumably I will have to live here too. If there were any place else available——"

"But there isn't," Mr. Hollins cried. "Is there, Mr. Smiley? Not another place available in this part of California, so close to the beach!"

"Not at this rent," Mr. Smiley boomed. "At the price it's a bargain, Mrs. Hollins, it's a steal. Of course, if you want to go to three hundred a month, maybe four hundred——"

"Out of the question, entirely out of the question," Mr. Hollins sang. "Tell me, is it for sale perhaps?"

"For sale?" Mr. Smiley shook his head. "Not on the market, Mr. Hollins. Owner doesn't want to sell. Lives up in Seattle now. Retired hardware man—name of Wilson. Came here for his health four, five years ago—just like you. Bought the house and moved in. But then he and Mrs. Wilson broke off. They quarreled, and she went off to live with a sister in Texas."

"Texas?" caroled Mr. Hollins. "Wonderful place, Texas. Big. Rugged. But not like California. So he won't sell, eh?"

"He says maybe his wife will change her mind and come back to him," Mr. Smiley said. "He wants to keep the house in case she does. Sentimental. But maybe he feels different since I wrote him last. I can query him and see."

"Do," Mr. Hollins urged. "Do, Mr. Smiley, and let me know what he says. Meanwhile we'll rent it, eh, Jocasta? We'll move in tomorrow and begin a new life together, tra la, tra la!"

Mrs. Hollins cast him a glance.

"You've been acting very strangely ever since we left Philadelphia," she sniffed. "Could it possibly be, Andrew, that you think you're going to persuade me to stay here more than six months? Are you toying with some idea of reviving that ridiculous hobby of painting pictures you had when I married you and made a successful business man out of you?"

"Painting pictures?" Mr. Hollins looked vastly surprised. "You mean my little notion that I wanted to be an artist? Why, whatever gave you such a thought, my pet? You showed me years ago how impractical the whole idea was. No, no—but I do like it here and I do think that maybe you will too. Six months it shall be if you insist, but I wager in the end you will change your mind and stay."

Mrs. Hollins' lips tightened.

"Not I," she said. "I promised you six months in California—

then we go back to Philadelphia. And never mind asking the owner if this place is for sale, Mr. Smiley. Six months is all we're staying, not one minute longer."

"You'll see, my dear, you'll see," Mr. Hollins promised gaily. "Listen to those waves, just listen to them, boom, boom, boom! And a furnace to keep us warm in case the air turns chilly!"

They moved in the next day. Familiarity, however, did not reconcile Mrs. Hollins either to the California climate, which remained unseasonably cloudy, or to the house. Although soundly built, it was undeniably damp.

"You'll have to start that furnace you're so proud of, Andrew," she said abruptly a few evenings later. "I'm getting a chill. This house will be the death of both of us, I know it will."

"It seems quite comfortable to me, my pet," Mr. Hollins answered from behind his newspaper. "But I'll light a little fire if it'll make you feel better. Perhaps it is the teeniest bit damp, now that you call my attention to it."

"It isn't just the dampness," Mrs. Hollins said darkly. "There's something wrong with this house. At night as I lie awake I can *feel* it. Something we don't know about."

"Tut, tut," chirped Mr. Hollins as he rose to go down to the cellar. "Mustn't let your imagination get the better of you. Perhaps you'd better give up those mysteries for a while."

Once in the cellar, Mr. Hollins set about making a fire, and soon had the furnace roaring merrily. He peered for awhile into the cherry-red firebox, as if thinking. Then he took a turn about the cellar, absently kicking the dirt floor with his toe. After some thought he fetched a spade and proceeded to dig a rather large hole in the corner behind the furnace. It did help, principally by concentrating all the moisture in one place. He continued until Jocasta called down to inquire what was keeping him. Then he put away the spade, rolled down his sleeves, and went back upstairs to his paper.

The next day the sun came out at last. But, curiously, neither sunlight nor warmth altered the atmosphere of the house, at least for Mrs. Hollins.

"Andrew," she said again the next evening, "I do not like this house. We must move."

"But we've signed a lease, pet," Mr. Hollins murmured, studying the baseball news. "Six months."

"We'll get out of it. Trust me to find a way."

"It's a very tight lease."

"We can break it. I shall find an excuse. I really believe I will write Mrs. Wilson, the owner's wife, and ask her about the history of this house. I'm sure there's something discreditable about it, and of course *he* would never tell us. If I'm right, it'll be excuse enough to break the lease. . . . Did that real estate agent say she was living in Texas now?"

And off she went to her writing desk.

The next afternoon Mr. Hollins drove to the village to inquire if Mr. Smiley had heard from the owner.

"Any day now." Mr. Smiley rubbed his hands. "Any day now. Like the place, do you?"

"My nerves are much better already," Mr. Hollins said. "But Mrs. Hollins does not seem to care for Villa Vista. She keeps threatening to go back to Philadelphia."

"Been saying around town she didn't like it," Mr. Smiley agreed. "Came in this morning wanting the address of Mrs. Wilson, the owner's wife. Should have heard her when I said I didn't know it, couldn't help her any."

He shook his head.

"Women!" he said. Mr. Hollins nodded and they both smiled.

The next morning Mr. Hollins went down into the cellar to inspect his drainage hole. After some thought he deepened it a good deal. When he had finished, he called his wife down to see.

"I do believe the water's draining away down into the hole," he said. "I think I hit a crevice that is carrying it away."

Mrs. Hollins peered into the excavation.

"Just imagination, Andrew. In any case, I repeat, we are not staying here. You'll see. Now fill the hole up again. The odor is quite nasty."

"Very well," Mr. Hollins agreed. "I'll fill it up."

And having raised the spade above his head, he brought it down with considerable force.

Into the hole tumbled Mrs. Hollins. For a moment her toes beat a brief tattoo; then with a final quiver she was still. She made no outcry, not a sound, not a murmur. And if she had, who was there to hear? The waves, the seagulls, the pebbles on the beach?

An hour later Mr. Hollins had the hole filled up. He tamped the earth down firmly. Previously he had mixed a small amount of cement with it, and in a short time the ground was almost as firm as rock.

He washed the tools and put them away. Then he packed Mrs. Hollins' trunks, carefully including everything, even her jewelry. Finally he took the trunks into the village in his car and at the railroad station arranged to send them back to Philadelphia.

The address on the tags, however, was that of a large storage warehouse. He had already written to arrange for indefinite storage.

Next he dropped in on Mr. Smiley.

"She's gone," he said. "Couldn't talk her out of it. We had rather a quarrel and she left me. I doubt if we shall ever make it up."

Mr. Smiley shook his head.

"Women just don't like that house."

"Perhaps the house just doesn't like women," Mr. Hollins suggested, rather wittily.

Pleased with the remark, he returned to Villa Vista and prepared supper for himself. Then he enjoyed an excellent night's sleep.

Next day, Mr. Smiley appeared while Mr. Hollins was finishing lunch.

"Got a phone call from the owner," Mr. Smiley said. "Just an hour ago. He's willing to sell now. For cash. Seems he's in a little legal trouble and needs the money to hire a lawyer."

He mentioned a price. Humming to himself, Mr. Hollins signed the purchase papers and made out a check.

When the real estate agent had gone, Mr. Hollins went happily to his writing desk. He got out paper and pen and happily began to make a list of the supplies he would need to take up again his long interrupted, but never forgotten, ambition to be an artist. Canvas . . . easel . . . brushes . . . paints . . . stretchers . . . turpentine. . . . It was a long list and he wrote down each item carefully, giving a little contented whistle as he worked.

When he had finished it was tea time. Happily he made himself tea, and did not mind in the least that he had to drink it quite alone. Jocasta's voice, that had rung in his ears for twenty-five years, was silent now, deliciously silent, beautifully silent. Never had silence sounded so golden!

After tea, Mr. Hollins strolled to the village to leave the list, to be filled and delivered. He returned home along the beach, breathing deeply of the salt air, watching with delight the play of the waves, the swoop of the gulls. Several times he skimmed pebbles into the briny water and once rescued a small fish that had become stranded on the beach.

When he reached the house, he paused.

The sheriff and two burly assistants were waiting there for him, with pickaxes and shovels.

"Didn't want to break in, Mr. Hollins," the sheriff said, "not having a warrant. Guess you'll let us in, though? Won't stand in the way of the law?"

"No," Mr. Hollins said, after a long moment. "No." He unlocked the door. "Come in, sheriff."

"C'm in, boys. . . . This the way to the cellar?"

"No, that's the coat closet. This is the door."

"Go ahead, boys. You know where to dig."

They disappeared. Presently from below came the thud-thud of pickaxes.

"Perhaps you'll tell me how you knew?" Mr. Hollins asked then, patting his brow with his handkerchief. "I really can't imagine how——"

"Your wife. Great little head on her. She told us yesterday."

"My wife—told you *yesterday?*"

"At first we thought it was just a woman's imagination. You know how women are, get a notion in their heads and get all worked up over nothing." The sheriff chuckled. "That's what we thought she'd done, at first."

"I'm afraid I don't understand." Mr. Hollins' face was pale.

"She didn't tell you? Why, she tried to write to Mrs. Wilson— you know, the owner's wife, used to live here."

"Yes—yes, I know."

"Well, she couldn't find any change of address for Mrs. Wilson at the post office. She was supposed to be in Texas—but all mail was forwarded to Mr. Wilson in Seattle, regardless."

"No change of address? But what——" Mr. Hollins began.

"What of it? That's what we said. And your wife lit into us." Another chuckle. "Yes, sir! She said any fool would know that a woman who left her husband wouldn't let him get her mail—she'd put in a change of address so she could get it herself. That proved, she said, Mrs. Wilson was dead. And if she was dead, Mr. Wilson must have killed her and made up the story about her leaving him."

"Wilson!" The word came from Mr. Hollins like a great cry. "*He* killed his wife?"

"That's right. Like I say, your wife kept after us until, by George, she convinced us. I wired Seattle last night, and the police went out to question Wilson. He thought we'd found the body so he broke down and admitted everything. He killed his wife, all right, just like your wife suspected, and buried her right in this cellar, extra deep, in the corner behind the furnace. . . . Where is Mrs. Hollins, anyway? I want to congratulate her."

The Vanishing Passenger

As stories of crime and detection are highly popular at the present time, I have decided to resume my literary career to chronicle the misadventures of my nephew, Jonathan Duke.

Though I have not appeared in print since 1929, my experience well fits me to chronicle Jonathan's escapades. I am the author, under the pseudonym The Duchess, of no less than forty-five full length romances, all published between 1914, when I first took up my pen, and 1929, when a fickle public taste deserted me.

My decision came to me while Jonathan and I were on our way to Hollywood on the Twentieth Century Limited. My forty-first volume, *No Kisses For Kathie,* was to be filmed with Jonathan playing opposite Miss Bette Bunton.

For fifteen minutes Jonathan had been yawning as he leafed through the script. I was not surprised when he put it down.

"Duchess," he said, "let's pay a visit to the club car and see what we can pick up—in the way of refreshments, I mean."

"You should be studying the script, Jonathan."

"It's tripe, Duchess, and besides it has to be rewritten."

"Of course it's tripe," I said stiffly. "But they paid me thirty thousand dollars for it. And they agreed to feature you in it."

"As a singing detective! Who ever heard of such a thing? Besides, there's no such character in the book!"

"None of the characters are the same. And the plot is different, too. I dislike quibbling, Jonathan. It's time you started a full-fledged career, and this is your opportunity."

"I suppose so," he agreed, giving the passing scenery a glance of ill-concealed distaste. "We'll talk about it in the club car."

It was in the second car from the club car that we met the girl. She was small, with dark brown hair, piquant features and a curvature of figure which Jonathan once described as "dynamic landscaping." She stood in the narrow aisle, facing a stout, middle-aged gentleman who was trying to enter his drawing room. They were arguing, but as we approached he rushed past her and slammed the door. We could hear his final words:

"For the last time, Miss Andrews, no!"

The girl glared at the closed door.

"You old dodo!" she said. Then she turned and saw us. Jonathan recognized her. I should have known he would. Making the acquaintance of attractive young women is as close as he has yet come to a definite career.

Her name, I learned, was Peggy Andrews. Her father was the famous, flighty and extravagant theatrical producer, Malcolm Andrews. And a few moments later we were all seated in the club car, ordering refreshments, while Peggy told us the reason for her agitation.

A few months earlier, her father's most successful venture, "Song of Summer," closed in Chicago, after grossing two million dollars. In the final accounting a full hundred thousand was missing. The evidence seemed to indicate Malcolm Andrews had spent it, and his backers had sworn out a warrant for him. His trial was to begin in Chicago on the following morning, and conviction seemed sure.

The stout individual Peggy had been arguing with was Horace Harrison, a handwriting expert who was on his way to Chicago to testify.

"The old dodo!" Peggy said again, dark eyes flashing fire. "The entries that make Dad look guilty are forgeries. Harrison must know it—but he won't tell me whether he's going to testify they are or aren't. Says he's sworn to secrecy! They wouldn't let me in his office. So I hung around outside. When he took this train, I took it too. Today I managed to catch him leaving the club car. But he still wouldn't talk to me. You saw him slam the door in my face."

"A low, unfeeling type," Jonathan agreed.

"If I only knew what he was going to testify!" Peggy finished her drink. "Maybe he's going to say they *aren't* forgeries! He looks just dumb enough not to know a forgery when he sees one."

She stood up.

"I'm going to go back and make him talk to me!" she exclaimed. "We're only three hours from Chicago and it's the last chance. He'll talk to me now or—or answer for it!"

Refusing Jonathan's offer to go with her, she marched out.

"Duchess, if you ever write another book, there's a character for you," Jonathan commented. "Just like her father—generous, warm-hearted, impulsive and unpredictable."

I informed him that I was already thinking of using her in a detective story, and that I proposed to make him the central character. He stared at me in horror.

"But Duchess! I'm no hero! In the old days you'd have cast me as the ne'er-do-well character who always loved and lost to a better man!"

"Fortunately, Jonathan," I told him, "heroes of detective stories are allowed far more latitude now than in my earlier writing days."

"But look, Aunt Agatha——" he only calls me Aunt Agatha when definitely disturbed—— "it's not practical, that's all! Anyway, I'm not a detective."

"My dear Jonathan," I replied, "you are a detective as much as you are anything else. You haven't enough will power to stay out of other people's troubles. You would drop anything to involve yourself in trouble with which you have no remotest connection."

My nephew merely looked sulky.

"Furthermore, I have been studying the detectives of modern fiction carefully. You are not quite like any of them, which is an asset."

"I like to think I'm at least a little bit like Philip Marlowe," he retorted, wounded. "With just a touch of Ellery Queen and Perry Mason."

"You are neither hard-boiled, intellectual, nor blasé," I pointed out. "Although twenty-nine and at times definitely capable——"

"Thanks, Duchess, for that crumb of comfort!"

"You also are capable of being quite immature. Especially in the presence of young females."

"Young, attractive females, please."

"All young females seem to have *some* attraction for you——"

"*Touché!* Ah, Duchess, if I'd only known you when you were younger."

"——and you have certain physical and mental qualifications which, did you lack them——"

" 'Did you lack them'! There's the genuine Duchess of 'Gloria, Girl Reporter' talking!"

"——I should have been forced to invent and attribute to you. Your father, my dear brother Hector, was intelligent, restless, and an extrovert. Otherwise he would never have found an oil well in Texas, or married a young Italian opera singer.

You inherit his physique, mentality and restlessness——"

"And money. Don't forget that, Duchess."

"——and your mother's looks, complexion and voice. The combination irresistibly attracts three things—young women, old women and trouble."

Jonathan refused to answer but signaled a waiter. I rose to my feet.

"The air is stuffy in here. I am going out on the observation platform to work out the plot for my first story about you."

On the observation platform of the club car I had only made a few notes when a man's hat, whisking from nowhere, blew against the grilled gate across the rear of the platform and stuck there.

It was a dark gray hat with a narrow snap brim, as I observed by retrieving it. I re-entered the club car, intending to hand it to the conductor, and saw that Peggy Andrews had returned and was talking to Jonathan again. Once more she seemed agitated—even more so than before.

"He wouldn't answer when I knocked, Johnny!" I heard her say. "But I heard him! He was in the drawing room, all right, and he was moaning."

"Maybe he was having a private attack of appendicitis," Jonathan hazarded. "Something personal like that."

"He's just joking, my dear," I told the distraught girl. "We will go up with you to see what is wrong."

Mr. Harrison's drawing room was only two cars forward. As we approached it I distinctly heard a slight groaning behind the closed door of Drawing Room A.

"He *is* moaning, Jonathan! I can hear him. We may have to force the door!"

The conductor, coming through at that moment, was made a member of our group. He got out his master key, then made the surprising discovery that Drawing Room A was not locked.

"Then something is holding the door shut!" Jonathan exclaimed. He added his weight to the conductor's. The door gave an inch, and distinctly through the opening we all heard a low groan.

"Harrison's lying on the floor in front of the door!" my nephew exclaimed. He and the conductor gave another shove. The door opened wide enough for Jonathan to squeeze through, and in another moment he was able to swing it open from the outside. We saw Harrison, the handwriting expert, lying on his right side, his eyes open and staring up at us in desperate, wordless appeal.

"There's blood all over the floor," Peggy said faintly.

"And a knife in his chest," Jonathan added. "Harrison, can you hear me? We'll have to get a doctor here as fast as we can find one on this train."

The handwriting expert's lips moved. Words came from them, faint and far away.

"Woman—woman's voice——"

"Go on!" Jonathan urged. "Who was she?"

"Opened the door——" Each word was gasped as if it might be the last. "I thought—Miss Andrews—stabbed me."

His mouth remained open, moving desperately. Then he relaxed and became only a huddled figure on the bloodstained floor of the tiny room.

"He's dead," Jonathan said.

"We need a detective!" the conductor—his name was Stevens—blurted out. And added, quite unnecessarily, "This is murder!"

Then he uttered an exclamation and pounced upon a tiny bit of cambric that had become jammed beneath the door when it was forced open.

"A handkerchief!" he cried hoarsely. "A lady's handkerchief. It's bloodstained. It's got an initial on it—an A. You heard him say he heard a woman's voice! This is a clue, this is."

"It's not a clue." It was Peggy Andrews speaking faintly, her features pinched and white. "It's not a clue at all. It—it's my handkerchief. I must have lost it!"

Half an hour later in my drawing room, Peggy sat and looked pleadingly at Jonathan and myself.

"Johnny—Miss Duke!" she begged. "Please say you don't believe I killed him!"

"Of course you didn't!" Jonathan said warmly, and was rewarded by a flush of color in her cheeks. I smiled and nodded, but did not commit myself. The evidence was rather overwhelming. I had already tabulated it for future reference, to wit:

(A) Peggy had been very angry at Mr. Harrison—had, in fact, threatened him in our hearing.

(B) Harrison's dying testimony was that he had heard a woman's voice and opened the door. Then he had added "Miss

Andrews . . . stabbed me. . . ."

(C) We had searched the dead man's drawing room and found a rifled brief case. Obviously the papers referring to Peggy's father had been removed. For this, only Peggy would have had a motive—a very telling point.

(D) The handkerchief, which had apparently been used to hold the murder knife, and then had been dropped beside the body by accident, was Peggy's.

"Since you didn't stab Harrison, Peggy——" Jonathan paused to pull out a short briar pipe and light it——"somebody else must have. But who?"

"The little man!" Peggy said eagerly. "The little man in the gray suit!"

"What little man in what gray suit?"

"The one who pushed past us just as we all met outside Mr. Harrison's drawing room. A little man, wearing a soft, gray hat, pulled way down, and a gray suit."

"I do seem to recall some such man," my nephew admitted. "What about him?"

"He was interested in Mr. Harrison too! I told you that when I couldn't get in to see Harrison, I hung around outside his office? Well, I saw that same little man twice. He was hanging around too—and I'm sure he was watching for Harrison just as I was. I wondered when he passed us in the car where I'd seen him before. And that was it."

Jonathan was about to reply when Conductor Stevens entered, worried but determined. He had, he said, arranged for a wire to Chicago. We would be there in two hours, and would make no stop on the way. Detectives would meet the train there to take off Harrison's body, and the murderer.

"And I do mean Miss Andrews!" Stevens said, his lean figure inflated with authority and importance. "She killed him!"

"Perhaps," Jonathan said in his most suave manner. "And yet we have information that an old enemy of Harrison's is aboard this train."

"An old enemy?" Conductor Stevens sucked at one cheek suspiciously. "What's his name?"

"I don't know his name. He is a small man, wearing a gray suit and a gray hat. He's been on the train ever since we left New York."

"Can't be! If he had 'a' been, I'd 'a' seen him, and I ain't."

"But you must have!" Peggy cried. "We saw him ourselves, not fifteen minutes before Mr. Harrison was killed, right outside Mr. Harrison's door."

Conductor Stevens disappeared into the corridor, gave a hoarse shout, and a few seconds later re-entered, followed by his assistant, short, well-fed and red-cheeked, whom he addressed as Bill. Questioned, Bill nodded.

"I know the little geezer you mean. He's in Car 103, Drawing Room B."

"Why didn't you tell me this before?" Conductor Stevens demanded, to which Bill replied, "You didn't ask me, Len."

Following this interchange, we went at once to Car 103, between the one in which Harrison had been murdered, and the club car.

Drawing Room B was empty.

We all stood gawking at its emptiness, as if we had expected to find a murderer there, his hands stained crimson, patiently waiting for us.

"You're crazy, Bill!" Len exploded. "There's nobody in this room. Not even a bag!"

Bill, however, stuck to his assertion, backed up by the porter, that a small man in a gray suit had occupied the room from New York.

"Must have left the train at the last stop," he suggested. "Since he sure ain't here now."

"But that was half an hour before the murder!" Conductor Stevens said triumphantly. "So even if the fellow was an enemy of Harrison's, which nobody's proved yet, he couldn't be guilty if he left the train before the deed was did. Now could he?"

The porter, Bill and I nodded. Jonathan only looked unhappy, a sure sign that his mental faculties had at last been fully engaged in the problem. Peggy was on the point of weeping.

"Maybe he got off," Jonathan said decisively. "And maybe he didn't. We have to search the train for him."

Conductor Stevens approached this idea with reluctance. He only gave in when Jonathan pointed out in firm tones that should Peggy be arrested, and later proved innocent, a large damage suit against the railroad would surely be filed.

Assistant Conductor Bill, the porter, and Peggy, all of whom could identify the man in the gray suit, set off with Jonathan. I, since I had not noticed him, remained in the empty drawing room. Although I offered my services, Jonathan declined them.

I took the opportunity to make a few more notes, and was in the midst of these when after awhile Jonathan and Peggy returned. Peggy's face was white and strained.

"He's not on the train," Peggy said, her voice trembling. "We looked everywhere—even in the baggage cars and the express car."

"Bill and the porter went into all the drawing rooms and compartments, pretending to check tickets," Jonathan added. "The washrooms too. The little gray man has just pulled on his invisibility suit and disappeared."

"But he couldn't have gotten off!" Peggy cried. "I saw him just as we met. And we didn't meet until after the last stop. He *has* to be on this train."

Jonathan flung himself down on the seat opposite me and stared moodily at the passing scenery.

"Since we're assuming Peggy isn't the killer, we have to assume the little gray man is," he said. "We also have to assume he's on the train, otherwise he couldn't be guilty."

"Why couldn't he have jumped off?" I asked, since it seemed obvious to me that this was a perfectly good possibility—*if* the little man was guilty. I was not prepared to concede his guilt, in view of the facts which I have listed earlier, but for Peggy's sake I certainly wanted to find him.

"He jumped off," I pursued the thought, "and his hat came off and blew back to the observation platform."

I held up the hat which I had retrieved from the platform an hour earlier, just before we had discovered the unfortunate

Mr. Harrison in his death throes. Jonathan pounced upon the hat as I explained the circumstances.

"Size six and a half!" he exclaimed. "Soft felt, snap brim, dark gray! A small man's hat! Peggy, is this the hat?"

Peggy examined it doubtfully.

"I don't know," she confessed at last. "If it was a woman's hat now—but it looks the same."

"He jumped off," I repeated, having now worked the matter out in my mind. "And his hat blew off. He used to be an acrobat—in vaudeville. But since vaudeville died, acrobats haven't been able to get work. This one became a bookkeeper. He got work in Peggy's father's office, falsified the books—he was a forger too, of course—and when he learned that Harrison was studying the books, became fearful Harrison had spotted his forged entries.

"So he followed Harrison onto this train, killed him, then jumped off. Being an acrobat, he could leap off safely. And—well, there you are."

Peggy and Jonathan both stared at me in undisguised admiration.

"That's how it must have been, Johnny!" Peggy cried. "Daddy does have a lot of old show people in his office. And four or five of them are little men. Daddy's so short, vanity makes him hire men even smaller. And—yes, I'm positive some of them were in vaudeville. One of them could easily have been an acrobat!"

"Duchess," Jonathan said finally, shaking his head, "I can see why you were such a success with your books. You go straight to the core of a problem."

"I rather think I do, Jonathan," I agreed.

"But if he jumped off the train, how can we ever find him?" Peggy's face clouded. "And even if we do, we'll never be able to locate him in time to help Dad. Besides, maybe the police won't even look for him. There's the conductor's testimony, and he's so certain that I'm guilty!"

"And, most unfortunately," I was forced to add, "Harrison's dying words were 'Miss Andrews . . . stabbed me.' That's going to sound very bad to a jury."

"What he meant," Jonathan stated, "was, 'I thought it was Miss Andrews calling me. I opened the door. Someone stabbed me.' But he couldn't get all the words out."

Then he snapped erect.

"But Harrison also said, 'I heard a woman's voice.' That's it! That's the clue we've been overlooking!"

"How, Johnny?" Peggy asked.

"Look!" And Jonathan's hand darted to the heavy upholstery of the seat a little to one side of me. He plucked up something and held it for us to see—a woman's long, black hair, twisting gently in the air currents.

"A woman's hair! And, both of you, what do you smell in this compartment? A scent of some kind, isn't it?"

We both sniffed. There was indeed an exotic odor in the air.

"It's that new perfume, Wolf Call!" Peggy cried.

"And," Jonathan added, "neither of you are using Wolf Call, are you?"

Peggy shook her head. I waited expectantly.

"Then," Jonathan said, "this drawing room has recently housed not only a little gray man, but a brunette wearing Wolf Call scent. She must have been his accomplice, who got Harrison to open his door—whose voice Harrison mistook for Peggy's. And even though the little gray man may have jumped off this train, we can be pretty certain the brunette didn't. So all we have to do is find her."

"But how?" Peggy looked perplexed. "There must be a hundred brunettes on this train. We can't just go up to all of them and ask, 'Are you mixed up in a murder?' "

"We will do it by a process of elimination," my nephew announced. "Only a few brunettes will be wearing Wolf Call. You, Peggy, and the Duchess will go through the train and, er, scent out the prospects. I will follow and, ah—interrogate them."

The modern passion for economy of words prevents me from detailing subsequent events as I should like to. They were, however, most interesting, revealing as they did certain of Jonathan's methods of meeting attractive young women.

As a preliminary, Peggy and I walked through the whole train, observing and—yes, I am not so old-fashioned I cannot use plain Anglo-Saxon—smelling.

In the first car we found only one prospect—an attractive brunette of about thirty, wearing a light, low-necked summer dress and sitting by herself, doing her nails a vivid carmine.

From the end of the car Jonathan saw our signal that she was using Wolf Call perfume. We then retired to the vestibule, and slowly he approached her. The car lurched as he was opposite her. It threw him far over her seat, where he remained for a moment, steadying himself. Then he straightened, apologized quickly, and hurried on to join us.

"She's not the one," he said. "Next car."

In the next car were three brunettes, of varying ages, wearing Wolf Call perfume. But all had husbands and children, so Jonathan ruled them out.

The car following contained two young ladies using the scent, both attractive, one wearing large, horn-rimmed glasses, the other avidly reading a magazine bearing the title *Her Charm*.

The young lady reading was near the end of the car. Peggy and I pretended to be getting a drink of water while Jonathan approached her.

"Pardon me," he asked in his most charming manner, "are you Miss Wilson?"

The brunette put down her magazine and giggled.

"I have a message for her from a friend in the first car. She said Miss Wilson was in this car and was a very pretty brunette, so——"

Jonathan paused. The girl giggled again.

Jonathan sighed.

"Very sorry if I've made a mistake," he muttered, and moved on.

The girl stopped giggling and watched his departure with large, forlorn eyes. Then she too sighed, and took up her magazine again.

Jonathan progressed to the next prospect. This one was small and buxom and the odor of Wolf Call emanated from her to a distance of several yards, subtly seductive.

Peggy and I casually sat down in the unoccupied seat behind her as Jonathan began.

"Excuse me," he said again, with a smile that would have done credit to an insurance agent, "are you Miss Wilson?"

The girl nodded.

"Yes," she said huskily. "Lola Wilson, Mr.—ah . . ."

"Duke," Jonathan said, obviously taken aback. "Uh, Johnny Duke."

"Sit down, Johnny." A sultry warmth underlined the invitation. "I knew we'd met someplace. New York, wasn't it?"

"I— don't think so——"

"Then it must have been Chicago." The horn-rimmed spectacles came off, were folded with a snap and placed in an ornate bag. "There, now I can see you better, Johnny. I just wear 'em to keep off mashers."

"Uh—good idea." Somehow Jonathan found himself occupying the empty seat beside her, though he started to move away. "Can't be too careful."

"That's what I always say to Mabel. She's my roommate. I live at the Lakestone Hotel. Lola Wilson. Room 711. Ever been to the Lakestone?"

At this point I rose.

"I am afraid," I told Peggy, "that no good can come of this except perhaps some interesting new contacts for Jonathan. Tell him I'll be back in the observation car when he gets tired of, ah—asking questions."

Peggy, a look of scorn frozen on her features, made no reply.

Thoughtfully I made my way back to the club car and dropped into a seat beside a small, pleasant, somewhat elderly lady who was knitting a sweater. She wore steel-rimmed glasses and her hair, mostly gray with a few streaks of the original black, was done in an old-fashioned but becoming bun. I made a note to use her as a character in a story sometime. One meets so few really wholesome people these days!

"People are so exasperating!" I said aloud. She looked up with interest.

"Aren't they?" she agreed. "But that's human nature, I guess."

"There is a murderer, or at least a murderer's accomplice, on board this train, and no one can find her," I stated.

"My goodness!" She dropped a stitch as she stared at me. "You're joking, aren't you?"

"I am not joking," I answered. "If she could be found, I would have a perfectly good mystery story. But she won't give herself away."

"Well, I hardly suppose she'd want to give herself away just so you would have a story," my new acquaintance pointed out.

That was true, of course, but no consolation to me. Perhaps I was not in a mood to be reasonable.

"She is a brunette, she wears daring perfume—I can still smell the nasty stuff—and surely those should be clues enough for any detective who is destined to become a popular favorite," I complained. "But are they? No! At least, not for Jonathan."

"Gracious!" my companion exclaimed, thrilled. "It sounds just like a movie. Tell me about it."

So I told her. If the story was never to be written, at least

I should have had one interested listener.

She listened spellbound, and when I had finished, sighed deeply.

"Well, I never," she murmured. "You make me almost afraid to look around. The accomplice might be sitting right next to me."

"She couldn't be," I pointed out. "Since I'm sitting next to you."

"Oh, I know," she said quickly. "But you see, you might be the accomplice, or even the murderer, for all I know."

This thought kept me silent for some moments. I was just estimating whether it would be a usable ending for a story when Jonathan entered. He looked weary and annoyed. Peggy was not with him.

"The conductor locked her in a drawing room," he explained. "We'll be in Chicago in half an hour and he's taking no chances."

"I'm sorry, Jonathan."

"Well——" he shrugged. "I guess I'm not such a hot detective as you were trying to make out. So——"

Then he paused. There was a faraway look in his eyes, and his nose wrinkled like a rabbit's—a boyhood habit indicating extreme abstraction.

"Might as well have something cold." He came out of his abstraction abruptly. "Let me order refreshments for you and your friend—"

"Miss Collins," I supplied, for so she had introduced herself as we chatted. "My nephew Jonathan. Miss Collins lives in

Evansville. Her brother is a professor there. I'll have a ginger ale."

"Just lemonade for me," Miss Collins said pleasantly. "I'm afraid I'm rather old-fashioned."

"Right." Jonathan turned away to signal the waiter, lost his balance and came down with all his weight on Miss Collins' foot. The poor creature screamed shrilly—and followed the scream with a deep, bass oath that filled the car.

"You clumsy baboon! You stepped on my——" Then, her features livid, she recovered herself. Her hand plunged into her knitting bag. But Jonathan moved faster. He reached out and snatched at Miss Collins' Queen Mary hat and her old-fashioned bun. Both came off cleanly, revealing a round, close-cropped masculine skull beneath.

"Miss Collins" uttered an even more unlady-like oath, and his hand came forth from his knitting bearing an automatic.

Jonathan's toe caught the man's wrist expertly. The gun came down a dozen feet away. Then Jonathan dragged "Miss Collins" to his feet and struck him sharply in the jaw. "Miss Collins" went quite limp and Jonathan, blowing on his knuckles, bowed to me.

"There, Duchess," he said. "Wrapped up and delivered to you. One murderer, F.O.B.—Found On Board."

It was not until later, after we had reached Chicago and I had transferred my baggage to the connecting train, that I had a chance to question him.

"Jonathan," I demanded sharply, as we stood on the platform of my Pullman, ready to depart for the West Coast, "I still do not fully quite understand——"

"Elementary, my dear aunt," he said hastily. "The killer vanishes from a speeding train. But only an acrobat, and a young acrobat, could possibly disappear by jumping off. The man's hat you found had a couple of short gray hairs in it—therefore, not a young acrobat.

"But you were on the right track when you mentioned Andrews' former vaudeville friends. He had dozens of them. 'Miss Collins' was one—not an employee, though, but a backer of 'Song of Summer.'

"His real name's Vaughan and he used to be in vaudeville as —well, let's face it, a female impersonator. He took up forgery, mulcted his fellow backers, and shifted the blame to Andrews. Then he got wind of Harrison's investigations and became scared. He came on board, prepared to kill Harrison if it proved necessary and to destroy the evidence.

"He didn't jump out of the window, naturally—he just threw his hat out. The wind took it back to the observation platform, where you found it. A man's hat is awkward to get into a handbag that must hold a man's suit and a pair of shoes.

"Vaughan knocked on Harrison's door, using his feminine voice. Harrison opened the door, and was stabbed. Then Vaughan closed the door, hurried to his drawing room, changed into woman's clothes, put on a wig, doused himself with perfume, tossed his hat out the window, and went elsewhere.

"And that's the only way a man can safely vanish from a speeding train—by changing into a woman."

"But what about the brunette accomplice?" I asked.

"There was no accomplice. I knew all along the killer was a man impersonating a woman."

"Indeed. May I ask how?"

"Quite simple, Duchess." He grinned. "That long dark hair we found——"

"Yes?"

"One end of it, instead of having a root, which normal hair falling from a normal scalp would have, had a tiny dab of glue on it. In other words, it had to come from a wig."

"Oh." At times I feel Jonathan has more intelligence than I give him credit for. "But why didn't you tell us?"

"I was afraid you'd get too eager and give things away. As it was, you were content to stand back and watch me."

"Hmph." I gave him a reproving look. "Did you have to question *all* those young women *quite* so closely?"

"That was to give me a close look at them." Jonathan grinned. "You see, I had to check up carefully upon their real or apparent sex. All the ones I talked to really were women."

I'm afraid I snorted a bit.

"Well," I admitted, "that explains certain things. But Vaughan was wearing a gray wig made to look like an old-fashioned bun. And you were looking for a young brunette."

"A mistake on my part," Jonathan admitted. "You noticed that wig was very carefully made. It was mostly gray, with just a few strands of dark hair in it. By sheer chance, the strand I found in the compartment was one of the dark ones, which led to an error in my deductions. Luckily the Wolf Call clue was on the level."

"But even so—" I grabbed him by the lapel as the train began to move and he seemed to want to leave me—"I still don't see how in the end you came to suspect such a sweet, innocent-seeming character as gray-haired little Miss Collins."

"I should have guessed that with your instinct you'd sit down beside the killer!" he retorted. "But I didn't. However, little motherly 'Miss Collins' reeked of Wolf Call. It's a perfume for the young. No elderly lady whose brother is a professor would wear it. But Vaughan wanted a perfume to help his disguise, and he took what some salesgirl sold him.

"Having realized then that 'Miss Collins' must be the 'woman' we wanted, I stepped on his foot. Pain and surprise usually upset such an impersonation—and they did this time. That's all. The stolen papers were in his luggage, and they'll exonerate Peggy's father. I'll see you in Hollywood."

"Jonathan!" I cried, but he was already gone. He swung down to the platform and ran alongside the car for a moment.

"Hollywood!" I shrieked at him. "The picture!"

"Rewriting will take two weeks!" he called back. "Look for me then."

He was dropping further and further behind now.

"Meeting Peggy for dinner tonight. Got to buy her a present." His voice came more and more faintly, his figure receding down the platform. "What do you—think of—a big bottle of Wolf Call?"

I answered reprovingly, but the train whistle drowned me out.

Hard Case

Old man Morris was known as a hard case. When his only boy, Harry, was held up on his eighteenth birthday and shot while bringing back the sale money for an exceptionally fine lot of cattle, Old Man Morris showed no emotion. He made no threats, gave way to no grief, and when an investigation turned up no clue to the murderer's identity, he went back to carrying on the necessary work on his small and lonely ranch.

The killing of Harry Morris turned out not to be an isolated instance. In the year following it, three more men were shot down in the Cochino River country, and two of them were carrying money at the time. The third, a rancher named Ike Carter, who had just previously left a large sum in the care of a friend, was found with six bullets in his head and chest —indicating that the killer, failing to find the expected booty, had emptied his gun into his victim in a fit of vicious temper.

But this was a slim clue to his identity, and no more revealing one was uncovered. The sheriff was old, and his blood ran thin. He merely sat and fretted. His two deputies, Sam Parr and Joe Green, though willing, lacked the instinct of the man hunter. They were energetic and covered a lot of territory in their search, but in a year they still had picked up nothing pointing to the identity of the murderer. So men who had to transport money in the Cochino River country no longer traveled alone.

Old Man Morris, however, when fortune for the first time in his life smiled on him, made no concession to a lifelong rule by asking for or accepting help in guarding his wealth.

The good fortune consisted of an unexpected offer for a small parcel of Oklahoma oil land that had been his wife's. Long disregarded, it had taken on value, and the check Old Man Morris cashed in the Cochino Center bank, translated into greenbacks, made an impressive appearance.

Old Man Morris, as he had shown no emotion at bad fortune, showed none at good. He took the bills the cashier counted out to him, made a tight roll the size of his thumb, and snapped a rubber band around it. Buttoning the money into his shirt pocket, he spent the early part of the afternoon doing some necessary shopping, and then set out in his buckboard for the thirty-mile drive homeward.

The sheriff made a vain attempt to get him to leave the money at the bank, since the whole county by now knew about it, or at least to get someone to ride along with him for protection. Old Man Morris was stubborn and, shaking his head direly, the sheriff gave up. With no protection except an ancient ten-gauge shotgun, carrying a charge of buckshot sufficient to tear a man in half, the old rancher slapped his team across the flanks and got under way.

He was three hours out of Cochino Center, crossing an alkali barren with night only an hour or so off, when the figure of a man on horseback appeared ahead of him.

Old Man Morris reached for his shotgun. Then, coming closer, he saw that the man was Sam Parr, the sheriff's deputy, and he relinquished his hold on the weapon.

Sam Parr held his place until the buckboard came up. Then he walked his horse alongside.

"I had a tip a stranger had been seen along this flank of Hermit Mountain," he told Old Man Morris. "I mentioned it to the sheriff, and he asked me if I'd mind coming out to scout around a bit, and sort of see you past this stretch anyway. I came over the Rocky Trail while you were pulling around. Haven't seen sign of anyone, though."

"Thanks," Old Man Morris said laconically.

"Town talk's you have a whale of a lot of money on you. You ain't afraid to be carryin' it alone through this country?" Sam Parr asked curiously.

"Why should I be?" the rancher asked. He touched the shotgun beside him. "I got old Andy Jackson here. Buckshot loaded. Blow a man in half." He paused, spat to one side into the alkali. "Has, too."

"But suppose this fellow who's been doing these killings waylaid you?" Sam Parr persisted. "Shot you from behind a rock, like he did your boy Harry?"

At the mention of his son, Old Man Morris's faded blue eyes took on a dark and angry color, but his seamed features did not alter and his tone was even.

"Wouldn't do him no good," he said. "I got my money hid. Hid where no living man is going to find it."

"You mean along the trail?"

The rancher shook his head.

"You mean on you?"

Old Man Morris nodded. "You could look for a week and not find it," he said, not boastfully but as a man stating fact. Then he added, "But Harry wasn't waylaid. He was shot from close up. There were powder marks on his face. He was shot by somebody he knew, and didn't suspicion, or he wouldn't 'a' let them get so close."

The team's hoofs sounded louder. A moment later the wheels of the buckboard were rattling over a long rocky outcropping. Sam Parr had pulled his horse casually to the right of the vehicle. Abruptly now he reined up close to Old Man Morris, and before the rancher could guess his intentions had drawn the .45 in his holster.

"You're right about that, old man!" he exclaimed, his tone

changing. "I shot him. Keep your hand away from that shotgun!"

Old Man Morris drew back his hand. Sam Parr leaned over and jerked the shotgun from its brackets, sat with it balanced across the horn of his saddle.

"Now," he ordered, "fork over the money."

The old rancher made no move. The stare he gave the deputy was level.

"So it's you, Sam," he commented. "I wasn't sure. Didn't know but maybe it was Joe Green. Knew it had to be somebody Harry recognized and wouldn't suspicion. Figured it out you two boys had the best excuses for goin' and comin' without nobody keepin' track of you."

"Never mind the gabble," Sam Parr told him curtly. "Hand over the money."

"Find it," Old Man Morris invited. "If you can." And he spat down onto the rock.

Sam Parr cursed. Then he dismounted, laid the ancient ten-gauge against a rock and, keeping the rancher covered with his .45, trussed him up with a coil of rope from the back of the buckboard.

After that he hunted for the money.

Forty minutes later, panting from his exertions, he quit. Old Man Morris' supplies were scattered across the rocky waste. The deputy had ripped open the flour sacks and spilled their contents, emptied the bags of coffee, and searched the beans and bacon. He had gone over the buckboard inch by inch, harness and all. He had of course searched the rancher first of all.

But he had found nothing. The roll of greenbacks Old Man Morris had got from the bank was still hidden.

Breathing heavily, his face flushed, the renegade deputy took up the shotgun and remounted.

"I want that money, Morris," he said between his teeth. "Tell me where you've cached it or I'll blow you all over the desert."

Old Man Morris shrugged as well as he could, considering the cocoon of rope he was wound in.

"Go ahead," he invited. "Shoot. But you'll never find the money. That's one thing you won't get."

Sam Parr's teeth clamped down. A little blue vein appeared in his forehead.

"By heaven, I will!" he bellowed.

He swung Old Man Morris' shotgun to his shoulder, braced himself for the kick of the heavily loaded old weapon, and pulled the trigger.

The ancient gun gave a tremendous roar, and belched a pall of smoke into his face. An instant later Sam Parr had been flung to the rock, and his horse was bolting.

Old Man Morris looked down at the mangled, bleeding man, twisting and moaning, and his expression did not change.

"I could prob'ly save your life, if I was free," he commented, beginning to squirm and wriggle inside his bonds.

The blast had gone off within inches of Sam Parr's face. But he could still form words with his lips.

"You——" he whispered hoarsely.

"Sure," Old Man Morris told him. "Me. I done it. I was laying for you. I knew I wouldn't never get no legal proof, so I baited a trap an' let you walk into it.

"You see, Sam, I knowed from the way the killer filled Ike Carter with lead when he found Ike didn't have his money on him that he had a crazy mean streak of temper in him. So I figured the idea of blowing me in half with my own shotgun would appeal to him when he got mad enough. Also, I knew if the killer was you or Joe, I wouldn't have no proof of it till too late to make a move myself. So I had to let you trap yourself, if I didn't want to risk shootin' the wrong man.

"Of course I knowed the shotgun would explode. Like I say, I figgered on it. What? How could I be sure you wouldn't find the money first, an' then just plug me an' ride off? Easy enough, Sam. I hid my roll in the barrel of the shotgun, just ahead of the charge. Bound to make the gun blow up in a man's face if it was fired."

The man on the ground tried to say something more, but the words would not come from a mouth that was half gone. A fresh gush of blood came instead, and Sam Parr fell back.

Old Man Morris, busy struggling with the knots that bound him, looked down on the dying man, his face expressing no emotion whatever.

The Cochino River country knew him as a hard case.

The Adventure
of the Single Footprint

Lieutenant Oliver Baynes of the State Police was squatting beside a footprint in a newly seeded section of lawn when I reached Hilltop, and a small photographer in large horn-rim glasses was capturing the print on celluloid, protesting bitterly against the tricky close-ups Baynes demanded. The job finished, he fled, but Baynes remained brooding over the print for a moment longer before he rose up to his full five feet seven.

"Thought there was a story here for you," he greeted me, his large red face solemn. "But it's a suicide verdict."

"It didn't sound like suicide over the phone. It sounded very fancy."

"I know." Baynes waved a hamlike hand toward the high wire fence that surrounded Lawford Holmes' hunting lodge and its five acres of well-treed grounds—grounds swarming now with State Troopers, local officers, and anyone else who could find an excuse to get in.

The fence was an impressive barrier. Ten feet high, it was topped by a V of barbed wire. All trees or brush within half a dozen feet on either side of it had been removed, and any overhanging branches that were low enough to touch it had been cut away.

"It's electrified," Baynes said. "The Holmes Gun people tested new small-arms models here during the war. A big alarm rings if the fence is cut or short-circuited or even touched. The system is guaranteed foolproof. The alarm didn't ring last night—so the fence wasn't tampered with. And there aren't any marks on the ground near it, either. Anyway, even if you used a ladder, you couldn't get over it without touching it and setting off the alarm.

"So it looks as if nobody from the outside got in here last night. And if nobody got in, Lawford Holmes wasn't killed. He shot himself."

"Then why are you so interested in this footprint?"

Baynes looked down at it. The footprint—only half a print, really, for it showed merely a deep toe indentation—was midway between two flagstoned walks some twelve feet from each other. Overhanging branches of a large pine had killed the lawn with shade, and a recent re-seeding had left the ground bare and slightly soft, or the print would not have registered. The grass beyond the walks was too thick to take an impression.

"The print wasn't here before last night," Baynes said. "The gardener swears to it, and he watered here at sundown. It was made by a man running toward the house. It's quite narrow, but it's just a toeprint, so it doesn't tell us much. It's the only evidence we've got that there could have been an outsider in these grounds last night. The other evidence says nobody could get through the fence without setting off the alarm, so the print must have been made by the gardener. But he insists it wasn't."

For a moment Baynes stood lost in thought, absently rubbing his bulbous nose with the side of his thumb. Then, for no reason, the mournful hoot of a freight train in the valley below made him nod. He turned toward the lodge where Lawford Holmes, president of the Holmes Gun and Iron Works, sat dead in his study with a Holmes bullet in his brain.

"Come on," he said. "You'll want to see the body, as long as you're here. Dead since about midnight, the doctors say. There was nobody here with him last night except the gardener and his wife, and the butler, Raymond, who make up the permanent staff."

"Why couldn't one of them have killed him?"

"The gardener and his wife went to bed at nine-thirty. They alibi each other and I believe them, because they had easy berths here and they had no motive. Raymond has been with

Holmes for fifteen years, and got a whopping salary for being discreet. He's out too."

"Somebody hiding here ahead of time?"

"He'd have been found this morning—the fence keeps people in just as effectively as it keeps them out. So that's not the answer. Anyway, Holmes drove up here unexpectedly yesterday, bringing only Raymond with him. On the way he stopped off at Glen Rest—that's the swanky sanitarium where his nephew Jack is locked up, crazy as a coot——"

"I know Jack Holmes," I interposed.

"You do?" Baynes's small blue eyes flashed me a glance. "Know him well?"

"We roomed together in college for a year. I was doing graduate work and was a good deal older, but we got along fine. I remember him as a tall, bright kid, good at debating and basketball. For some reason I always thought he'd go places."

"Know anything about him since college?"

"Just the highlights—his father's death here at Hilltop, Jack's war record, his wound, his mental breakdown after he got back —the kind of things you read in the papers."

"Mmm. Anyway, Lawford Holmes stopped to ask how Jack was doing, then drove on here. He got here at six and the fence was turned on right away."

"What was he afraid of?"

"Nothing in particular. Of course, he had enemies who wouldn't have minded killing him—former employees, business associates he'd cheated, the brother of a woman he was mixed up with—but none of them were on his trail so far as we know. He just liked to feel secure.

"He had dinner, then went to his study to read. Raymond left him there reading at eleven and went to bed. Sometime in the next hour, Lawford Holmes died. But nobody heard the shot or any kind of outcry. . . . Well, here's the house. It wasn't locked. Lawford Holmes depended on his electric fence."

We went up fieldstone steps, through an open door and down a wide hall, to turn into a small room with a picture window showing a breath-taking view of the Berkshire peaks across the valley. But the view inside the room stole the show.

Beside a reading lamp opposite the doorway was an easy chair, and in it sat an enormously fat man with porcine features. His head was rolled grotesquely to one side, the tiny eyes open and staring. The blackened area of a contact wound showed on his right temple.

As he slumped there, the dead man's arms dangled beside the arms of the chair. And just beneath each limp hand a .32 Holmes automatic lay on the rug.

"Raymond found him like that at eight this morning, the light still burning," Baynes said. "A pretty picture of a suicide, isn't it?"

"With *two* guns?" I exclaimed. "I've heard of two-gun killers, but I've never heard of a two-gun suicide before!"

"The left gun didn't fire. A defective bullet jammed in the barrel."

"You mean he tried it, the gun jammed, so he dropped it and

used another?" I asked. "Or what? Was it suicide or wasn't it?"

Baynes heaved a sigh.

"No," he said, "I don't think it's suicide. Not just on account of the two guns, or even the footprint. But it doesn't *feel* like suicide to me."

"But you haven't any evidence to prove different?"

"Just the footprint. And you might call this evidence."

He indicated the paneled wall beside the doorway. A few inches from the doorjamb there was a small indentation in the paneling. In the polished floor directly beneath was another dent, larger but shallower.

"The butler swears those weren't there yesterday."

"What do they mean?"

"Your guess is as good as mine." Baynes stared darkly at the dead man, so grossly different from his brother, Harrison Holmes, founder of the company. From his portrait on the wall above the fat man's body, Harrison Holmes looked down aloofly, tall, white-haired, fiercely honest.

"It'll go down as suicide," Baynes said, after a moment. "Just like his brother's death went down as an accident."

"Harrison?" I exclaimed. "Jack's father? He fell off a cliff here during the war. Are you trying to tell me he was murdered too?"

"I'm not trying to tell you anything. But during the war a big shipment of defective Holmes ammunition hit the battle-fields. Harrison brought his production chief, his brother Lawford, and some section managers up here for private questioning. Harrison fell over a cliff while he and his brother were out walking in the middle of that questioning."

"You mean Lawford Holmes was responsible for the bad ammunition? He killed his brother to keep the facts from coming out?"

"Nobody ever proved it. In fact, nobody was ever officially blamed for the bad ammunition. It just stopped appearing. But after his brother died, Lawford took over the company. Jack was in a hospital in Italy then, with a bad head wound. . . . He could have had a military exemption, but he enlisted. Rose to be a major."

I nodded. That side of Jack's history had been played up in the newspapers.

"What are you getting at?"

Oliver Baynes beamed at me. He has helped me get many a true crime story which I have written up, with a reward in publicity to him—and no official shuns publicity. But behind the face and figure of a bloated pixie Baynes hides the soul of a frustrated dramatist. He loves to be mysterious, as if to prove that life, properly stage-managed, can be more startling than any of my fictions.

"I'm trying to tell you how Jack Holmes got to be crazy," he retorted. "Didn't you ever wonder?"

"Yes, of course. I meant to make inquiries, but I never did."

"That's how it goes. Well, it was his uncle's fault." He gestured toward the dead man lolling mutely before us. "When Jack got out of the Army, a year after his dad died, Lawford was running the company. Jack tried to get the company back but this cute fellow had fixed the by-laws somehow, making himself practically the permanent president. Jack was licked.

"He began to brood. He suspected his uncle had killed his father, he was pretty sure Lawford had been behind the bad ammunition, and he knew he was trying to steal the company. And Jack couldn't do a thing about any of that. So he jumped his mental rails to get away from a conflict he couldn't resolve, and they had to lock him up."

"What form does his dementia take?"

"He thinks he's somebody he isn't."

"Who?"

"The other Holmes."

"What other Holmes? Oliver Wendell?"

"Not Oliver Wendell, no. I thought you mystery writers have only one Holmes."

"Wait a minute!" I cried. "You don't mean he thinks he's——"

"That's right." Baynes chuckled. This was the moment he'd been leading me up to. "He thinks he's Sherlock Holmes in the flesh."

"But that's——" I'd been about to say, "That's impossible!" But of course it wasn't. Plenty of people think they're Napoleon or Julius Caesar or Genghis Khan.

"It's perfectly natural, according to the doctors," Baynes went on. "As a boy, Jack was tall, skinny, and eagle-beaked. His full name is John Sherwin Holmes. What else could the other kids call him but Sherlock?

"He liked it. He boasted that Sherlock Holmes was a relative. He read all the stories and made up plays about him and acted in them. Of course, it was just a game and he outgrew it. But when he came back from the war, shaky from his wound and combat fatigue, he ran head-on into his uncle and found himself helpless. So mentally he retreated to his carefree boyhood. Instead of being John Sherwin Holmes he became somebody else—somebody big and important. Sherlock Holmes."

"Good Lord!"

"I was wondering—how'd you like to call on him this afternoon?"

"Call on him? Why?"

Baynes glanced again at the gross figure of the dead man so close to us, seeming to stare at us out of tiny pig eyes that saw nothing.

"There's nothing more we can do here," he said. "But maybe if we call on Jack, we can make his uncle cure him."

"But his uncle's dead! How can he cure Jack?"

"By being dead," Baynes answered.

Glen Rest covers fifty acres in the Berkshires some forty miles south of Hilltop. A large central building that might be a summer resort is surrounded by individual cottages, each on its own grounds. Inmates who are merely rich are kept in the main building. The cottages are for those who are more than rich and who are, of course, non-violent.

Most of the inmates are permitted to move freely through the grounds during the day, accompanied by attendants. Restraint is imposed by a high brick wall, patroled day and night by guards who travel in pairs. But the guards remain unobtrusive and the wall is screened by trees and flowering shrubs. The resort atmosphere is seldom disturbed and any harmless whim within reason is indulged.

At Glen Rest, as Baynes observed, you can live in your own private Mount Vernon if you think you're George Washington and ride around on your own white horse if you think you're Paul Revere.

We reached there late in the afternoon, driving down from Hilltop in Baynes' car after Baynes had bullied the small photographer into rushing through a comprehensive set of photographs for him. When we left, the activity within the fenced-in grounds had ceased; no evidence of murder other than the single footprint had been found.

At Glen Rest Baynes disappeared for twenty minutes into the main office. Then we drove on to a small, English-type cottage two hundred yards away. Maples surrounded it, and in the backyard stood a dozen beehives.

"This is where they keep Jack," Baynes said, stopping. "He hasn't been out of the grounds in more than a year now—I just asked. And he hasn't seen his uncle since he was admitted. Lawford stopped in from time to time to ask about him, but the sight of his uncle made Jack so violent that the two were never permitted to meet."

"Now perhaps you'll tell me what crazy idea you have for curing him?"

"It's not crazy. The doctors okayed it. You see, his uncle is the immovable object Jack ran into. As soon as he learns his uncle is dead, and the obstacle no longer exists, he may snap back to normal."

"Then why not wait and show him a newspaper clipping telling of his uncle's death?"

"That's too direct. The unbalanced mind throws up defenses against evidence from the normal world. So I'm going to sneak up on his blind side."

"I don't follow you."

"It's like this. I'm calling on Jack now as Inspector Baynes of Scotland Yard, coming to ask Sherlock Holmes for help on a case—the murder of Lawford Holmes, a distant family connection."

I reacted in a manner to satisfy even Baynes' sense of drama. Then I added: "It might work—if he's crazy enough to believe your story about wanting his help."

"He'll believe it. I've dropped in before, using cases that were bothering me as an excuse. Darned if he didn't give me a couple of suggestions. Outside his delusion, or inside it rather, his mind clicks fine.

"I got interested in him more than a year ago because I'm partly responsible for his being here. I was out on a patrol with one of our troopers when a car passed doing eighty. Jack was at the wheel. He told us he was Sherlock Holmes, and was testing the comparative speed of different motorcars for a monograph he was writing on automotive vehicles and their uses in apprehending criminals."

"I'd like to have seen your face!"

"I thought he was being wise. But when he learned my name, he fell on me like a long-lost brother. It seems there's a Baynes in one of the Sherlock stories."

"That's right. Inspector Baynes in *The Adventure of Wisteria Lodge*. A smart officer."

"I know, I read it. Anyway, we took Jack home and a month later he was here at Glen Rest. He used to have lucid intervals but now the slightest suggestion that he's not the real Sherlock Holmes sets him off into a kind of fit. So we have to be careful."

"I'll be careful. But just what do you want me to do?"

"You're going to play Dr. Watson."

"Dr. Watson!"

"That's right. You're blond, pudgy, and English-looking, and he'll remember you as an old friend and accept you. But you haven't seen him since he left London. You see those beehives out back?"

"Yes. Good Lord, you mean he's——"

"He's retired. This is his cottage in Sussex, where he's raising bees. His nurse-housekeeper is Mrs. Hudson, who's come down from London to look after him. Now we're going in. Just be Dr. Watson—ask questions and make remarks that aren't too bright. But remember, play it straight."

(We did "play it straight." Consequently I have taken the liberty, in the following section of these notes, of writing it "straight"—to keep the narrative from becoming hopelessly confused between our real and assumed identities.)

Upon Baynes' knock the cottage door was opened by Mrs. Hudson, whose pleasant face brightened as she saw us.

"Come in, Inspector Baynes!" she exclaimed. "And Dr. Watson! Mr. Holmes has been waiting ever since your phone call. He said to show you into the study."

Mrs. Hudson rustled starchily ahead of us into a small, incredibly cluttered den.

"I'll call Mr. Holmes right away," she said. "He's out in back with his bees—trying out what different vitamins will do to the honey."

She rustled out again, and I seized the opportunity to inspect the books and papers which spilled from shelves all around the room and teetered in Pisan towers on the floor. Holmes had always been an omnivorous reader, and it was evident the habit persisted even here, for the books I saw covered twenty different subjects or more.

All the newspapers and magazines were English. Sheets of foolscap covered with a large, flowing handwriting were strewn across the desk. Two books lay open across them, as if recently consulted: Sheldon's *Varieties of Human Physique* and *Varieties of Temperament*. More I had no chance to observe, for footsteps came down the hall and an instant later Holmes himself came in. He wore old tweeds and was engaged in removing beekeeper's gloves and helmet, which he dropped carelessly into the middle of the room.

"Watson!" he cried, seizing my hand in a crushing grip, the well-remembered features breaking into a smile. "Forgive my exuberance, but I have few visitors, and the country air has improved my health so much that I can hardly find an outlet for my energies."

He flung himself into an old Morris chair and pulled open the door of a cabinet beside him. I could see now that his face was thin and haggard, looking older than his years warranted, and there was a certain glint of wildness in his eyes which had never been there before. Otherwise, he was hardly changed from the last time I had seen him.

"Watson—Inspector Baynes," he said, drawing a bottle, three glasses, and a seltzer-maker from the cabinet. "You'll have some refreshment, I'm sure. You've had a long trip and no doubt you've talked yourself dry about the case on the way down."

"Case?" I asked. "What case, Holmes?"

"I can hardly tell that yet. But since you have prepared yourself with a folded wad of copy paper in one pocket and four sharpened pencils in the other, you certainly plan to take notes. And if not of a case which you hope to write up, then of what?"

"Oh, of course," I muttered. Baynes grinned at me. Holmes poured out three drinks and added a squirt of seltzer to each.

"Quite an improvement over the old gasogene, eh, Watson?" he remarked as he handled the gleaming sodamaker. "Which you were always secretly afraid would explode. . . . Well, gentlemen, to use that prevalent Americanism which so aptly covers our mutual interest, here's to crime!"

We all drank, and Holmes turned to Inspector Baynes.

"I grant you, Baynes," he said, "that the case is baffling, colorful, and important. But really, I cannot undertake it. I am retired."

"But you don't know yet what case we've come to consult you about, Mr. Holmes!" Baynes protested.

"It must be colorful, or Watson would not deem it worthy

of his talents," Holmes remarked, directing a glance at me. "Baffling, or you would not be here, and important, or you would not have gone to the length of bringing Watson along to exert pressure on me to take it. But the day of the individualist in crime detection is past. Modern criminology is the science of massed attack. Whole regiments of men at telephones and microscopes, whole armies of girls at filing cabinets—today they net the malefactor. The few carefully selected facts with which the individual craftsman can work are puny artillery indeed in modern warfare against crime. I've outlived my day, and I'm wise enough to know it."

"I was afraid you'd feel like that, Mr. Holmes," Baynes said regretfully. "But just the same, I hope you'll help me out. For one thing, this case involves, I believe, a distant family connection of yours."

"Indeed?" The massive eyebrows rose, the hawknose flared. "My family connections are scanty enough. Which, pray, do you refer to? And is the individual the malefactor or the victim?"

"I'm speaking of Lawford Holmes, the munitions maker," Baynes said. "He's been murdered."

"Murdered?" Holmes' face lit up. The wild expression seemed to leave his eyes. "Yes, I believe Lawford Holmes is a connection, though I've never traced the exact degree of consanguinity. When did he die?"

"Last night, at his lodge, about forty miles from here."

"Tell me about it, my dear Inspector." Holmes leaned back, filled an ancient briar, and lit it.

Baynes then went into a careful, detailed recital of the circumstances of Lawford Holmes' death. Puffing at his pipe, Holmes listened, following the narrative carefully. Baynes emphasized the absence of clues, save for the single half-footprint and the two dubious dents in the library woodwork. When he had finished describing the position in which the dead man's body had been found, with a recently fired gun beneath his right hand and one with the barrel jammed beneath his left, Holmes sat up and knocked the dottle from his pipe.

"Curious!" he remarked. "Decidedly curious! Several possibilities present themselves, each with a certain appeal. How do you read this riddle, Watson?"

"I see nothing in the facts that establishes murder at all," I replied. "Since it looks so much like suicide, why can we not assume it *was* suicide?"

"And how do you explain the second gun, the one that jammed?" Holmes asked, watching me with a slight smile.

"Possibly Lawford Holmes was examining it—it may have been left over from the investigation into the defective ammunition which the factory issued," I answered. "He may have suddenly felt remorse for sending brave men to their death with other such faulty bullets, and thereupon killed himself."

"Bravo!" Holmes applauded. "An ingenious theory, entirely worthy of you, Watson. But better suited to literary than practical purposes, I fancy. And what, Baynes, is the official theory—for I assume that the authorities have arrived at some conclusion?"

"The official explanation," Baynes said gloomily, "is that in a freakish mood of despondency Lawford Holmes decided to kill himself by firing two shots into his head simultaneously, with a gun in each hand. One gun fired and the other jammed, accounting for their positions beside his chair."

"Ingenious, decidedly ingenious!" Holmes agreed. "But you don't believe it, eh?"

"No, I don't believe it. Lawford Holmes wasn't the kind of man to kill himself. But now if you're going to ask me *my* theory, Mr. Holmes, the best I can do is say that it looks to me like a vengeance murder. The killer may have been a former serviceman whose life was endangered by defective Holmes ammunition. Or he may have lost a buddy, killed on account of a jammed gun.

"So he brought back the useless gun with him, determined to have vengeance on the man responsible—in this case, Lawford Holmes, head of the company. Having killed his man and made it look like a suicide, he dropped the other gun as a subtle sign of justice accomplished."

"A distinct possibility," Holmes acknowledged. "That is, if— was either gun an Army-issue weapon?"

Baynes' face fell.

"No," he admitted. "That's the trouble with the theory. The gun that killed Lawford Holmes was his own, commonly kept in his desk drawer. The other is untraceable. It has no serial number and apparently was removed from the factory before being stamped. Of course, Lawford Holmes himself could easily have got hold of an unnumbered gun—so we're back to the suicide theory again. But I don't believe it," he finished doggedly.

"Neither do I. The Holmes blood line is an aggressive one, not given to suicide, as you rightly remarked. Well, Baynes, you have an intriguing puzzle on your hands. It would interest me to attempt it, but I must not let myself be tempted. I have retired. I'm sure you will succeed without my help."

"I wish I could be as sure," Baynes said wryly. "The trouble is, I've only the footprint and the two dents in the woodwork, and I'm afraid they aren't clues enough."

"A slender stock, I agree. But even a single footprint, my dear Baynes, when studied with sufficient care has been known to reveal volumes."

Baynes brightened. "Perhaps you'd be willing to look at it for me?" he suggested. "I don't mean necessarily to go to the scene, but I have a very good photograph with me."

Holmes hesitated, and I swiftly interposed: "Surely it can do no harm to glance at a photograph, Holmes. I daresay you can tell nothing from it, but why not look anyway?"

Holmes appeared, I thought, nettled.

"As you say, Watson, why not?" he agreed. "Let us examine, then, your picture of this single print, Baynes. And of the two small dents in the library woodwork, if you have pictures of them as well. It is conceivable we may extract something from them despite Watson's scepticism."

Baynes dug into the battered brief case he had brought with him and produced a handful of photographs, still slightly damp.

"I have pictures of the whole scene here," he said hopefully.

"The grounds, the house, the electrified fence, the position of the body——"

"No, no!" Holmes cried. "You are thorough, Baynes. When you say there are no other clues, I have confidence in the statement."

Thus restrained, Baynes dug through the photographs, selected six, and handed them to Holmes. Three showed the single footprint—a close-up and two general views of the surrounding grounds. The other three showed the small dents in the library woodwork, both in close-up and from a distance of a few feet.

To these latter Holmes first applied himself, taking a large reading glass from the desk to assist him. Presently he passed them to me and sat back, drumming the tips of his fingers against the arms of his chair.

"Suggestive, most suggestive," he murmured. "What a deal of train-catching and hansom riding the art of photography could have saved us in our earlier days, had it been sufficiently advanced, eh, Watson?"

"Very possibly," I agreed. "But as for these marks being suggestive, to me they suggest nothing save a careless house-maid knocking a broom handle about."

"Come, Watson!" Holmes remonstrated. "Baynes says these marks did not exist prior to the murder. Then logic tells us they must have been made during its commission, eh?"

"Well, yes, I suppose so."

"And two dents in highly polished woodwork, one on the wall, the other in the floor directly below—their position tells you nothing?"

"I suppose something hit the wall and fell to the floor."

"Bravo, Watson, we progress! Something heavy obviously. And something that was thrown. Nothing dropped accidentally could have made both marks."

"I suppose not. But what?"

"What indeed? Let us go back a bit. Whatever it was, who threw it? Who must have thrown it?"

"Why, Lawford Holmes, I daresay. His chair faced the door."

"Exactly, Lawford Holmes. And under what circumstances does one hurl heavy objects with reckless disregard for valuable woodwork? At an intruder, to be sure. Thus we establish that Lawford Holmes was not taken unawares, but did make an effort to defend himself."

"But what did he throw?" I demanded. "If the dents tell you so much, they must surely tell you that!"

"We do not need the dents for that information. What else could the dead man have thrown but a gun which, having failed to fire, was useful only as a missile? Eh, Baynes?"

"Very sound, Mr. Holmes, very sound indeed!" Baynes applauded.

"But that would mean Lawford Holmes actually had the gun in his hand when the killer entered!" I objected.

Holmes shrugged. "Not necessarily."

"I disagree!" I told him. "And if Lawford Holmes had the gun in his hand, that means he had some warning of the killer's approach. But in that case why didn't he take his other gun, customarily kept in his desk? Why didn't he ring for the butler or make an outcry? The gun having failed to fire, how was he killed so as to simulate suicide and without any sign of a struggle? How——"

"Softly, Watson, softly." Holmes held up a restraining hand. "You are beclouding the issue in complications. I can, however, suggest one hypothesis which answers all such questions."

"And what is it?" I cried.

Holmes pondered for a moment. Then he shook his head.

"No, Watson. In the absence of other data it must remain, after all, guesswork. And you know how I feel about guesswork. Further inference from these two small indentations must wait for the accumulation of more facts. Let us now turn our attention to the footprint which so interests Baynes."

So saying, he took up the photographs of the toeprint. For some minutes he studied them through his glass. Then he put them down.

"Well, this is more informative!" he exclaimed, obviously pleased. "You underestimated the value of your footprint, Baynes. While it does not tell us the guilty man's name, nor the color of his suit, nor, alas, his nationality or politics, I fancy it gives us otherwise a comprehensive view both of his person and personality, together with full information regarding his mode of entrance to and exit from the grounds."

"What?" Baynes straightened and stared at Holmes incredulously. "You can read all that in a picture of a footprint?"

"If it were a full footprint, instead of but half a one, perhaps I could read more," Holmes replied calmly. "Let us approach this photograph with only logic for our guide, and see what result we achieve. What have we? A toeprint in seeded ground, deeply indented. Our first postulate is that it was made by a man running swiftly. Do you agree?"

"Agree?" Baynes asked. "Oh, yes, I agree, Mr. Holmes."

"But the print indicates the man who made it was running *toward* the house, not away from it. Consequently he cannot have been fleeing. And you have said there was no outcry or alarm of any kind."

"That's right," Baynes agreed cautiously. "No, he couldn't have been fleeing."

"But there can have been no reason for him to run toward the house before the murder. His whole approach, as we visualize it, was one of stealth. Consequently his running was neither to flee nor to attack. For what other reason might a man conceivably run at high speed?"

Holmes paused, but neither Baynes nor I answered. After a moment he continued.

"One other possibility comes to mind," he stated. "He might have been running to gain momentum."

"Momentum?" I asked, blankly. "Why momentum?"

"Why, indeed? Let us examine the picture again. The shade of the overhanging branches of a pine tree has killed the lawn. One such branch is visible in the picture—some twelve feet, I estimate, directly above the print in question."

"Yes," Baynes corroborated. "Twelve feet is about right."

"Then our picture is complete!" Holmes exclaimed. "The toe indentation is really too deep to have been made by a man merely running. We can state confidently that he was not, indeed, running. He was *jumping*. The print, in fact, was made as our man leaped for that branch, twelve feet above the ground."

"Some jump!" I exclaimed.

"Some jump, as you inelegantly phrase it, Watson. Surely your English has become more Americanized in recent years? The effect of seeing too many gangster cinemas, I daresay. But a jump within the capabilities of an athletic man."

"But, if he did jump for the branch, why?" I asked. "Surely he wasn't going to hide in the tree?"

"Of course not. There was no alarm and no necessity to hide. But in this picture the branches of the pine interlace with those of another tree closer to the electrified fence. And those in turn—the photograph does not show it, but it must be so—interlace with other trees, extending to the other side of the fence. Our killer, then, came and went through the branches of the trees, climbing one on the outside, swinging through high *above* the fence, dropping into the grounds, and departing in the same manner once his mission was accomplished."

"You've hit it, Mr. Holmes!" Baynes exclaimed. "You've hit it! It's the only answer!"

"But it would take a Tarzan to do it!" I objected.

"Then a Tarzan we must postulate," Holmes said confidently. "As Baynes has said, it is the only answer logic permits."

"But you said, Mr. Holmes," Baynes put in, "that the print told you what our man looks like, and his personality too. You were just joking, I expect?"

"Joking?" Holmes repeated. "I never joke on such matters.

Let us pursue our analysis further. This single print is midway between two walks twelve feet apart. His previous step, we may assume, came upon a flagstone, otherwise it would have registered. Our man's running stride then is at least six feet— the stride of a tall man. Likewise it would take a tall man to make the leap to the branch in question. The toeprint is a narrow one. A narrow foot indicates small bones, a slender man. Equally, such a venturesome trip through the trees would be impossible to a man of great weight. Consequently we may say with confidence that our man is tall and slender. He is also, obviously, athletic."

Baynes shook his head in admiration.

"I thought there was nothing to be told by that print," he remarked, "but you have proved me wrong. But surely, Mr. Holmes, you can tell nothing more from it."

"Only a little," he said modestly. "Nothing in fact, save that in addition to being tall, slender, and athletic, the man you seek probably eats sparingly, does not enjoy strong drink, and occasionally suffers from nervous irritability and insomnia. I might venture to add that he probably plays bridge better than he does poker, is intelligent, capable of meticulous planning, but at the same time is emotional and even on occasion reckless. At times he is sociable and fond of athletics, but at other times will be moody and given to solitary pastimes. Beyond these small facts, however, I am unable to go."

"Come now, Holmes," I cried indignantly. "You're making that up. You cannot convince me that you can read a man's whole inner nature from his footprint!"

Holmes chuckled.

"I hesitate to reveal my reasoning," he said, "for fear you will find it too elementary, as you have sometimes in the past. But since I know you will insist, I shall endeavor to oblige.

"We know that our man is tall and slender. From the circumstances of the crime we can deduce his intelligence, his ability at planning, and certainly a quality of emotionalism and recklessness.

"The rest—his temperament, ability at bridge, dislike of strong drink, tendency to insomnia, and other trivia—I have taken almost verbatim from those two excellent studies by Sheldon, *Varieties of Human Physique* and *Varieties of Temperament*. There they are on my desk; I was studying them this morning.

"I saw you glance at them earlier, Watson. You should read them. Without going into detail, Sheldon has found that all mankind falls into certain physical types and subtypes. Each type, he has ascertained, has corresponding and predictable temperamental and physiological attributes.

"In this instance, given what we can legitimately deduce about our quarry, we can then place him in the group which, Sheldon has found, is liable to insomnia, to being upset by strong drink, and the rest. You see—simplicity itself."

Holmes rose.

"Though Shakespeare antedated Sheldon by several centuries, Sheldon's conclusions were not unknown to him. He said quite accurately of lean and hungry Cassius that 'such men are dangerous.' And in the immortal Hamlet he accurately depicted another murderer who certainly has a family resemblance to the one under our consideration.

"We seem to have used literary allusion liberally in describing him, have we not? Something of a Tarzan and something of a Hamlet—a mixed personality! But such you will find him, I feel sure.

"Now you'll be wanting to get about your job, eh, Baynes? When Sheldon's work is more universally known, it will be necessary only to detail all the facts of a crime, feed them into a computer, and presto! an accurate description of the criminal will emerge. But for now the police must do some work themselves.

"So I won't keep you any longer. Please let me know how you make out. I'll await the result with interest. And Watson, come again, do. Sooner this time, if your good wife will let you."

So we were dismissed. My last impression was of the tall, lean figure in the doorway, deep-set eyes glinting as one sinewy hand waved good-bye. Then the door closed and *The Adventure of the Single Footprint* was over.

Baynes was silent as we drove away from Glen Rest. My own comments drew forth only noncommittal grunts until after we had reached my summer cottage. Then Oliver Baynes settled back and regarded me moodily.

"All I can tell you from this footprint," he misquoted, "is that your killer is tall, thin, athletic, intelligent, emotional, has insomnia, doesn't like hard liquor, and plays a good game of bridge."

"You're not taking what Jack said seriously?"

"Of course I'm taking it seriously! It's right, every word of it!"

"But Jack's out of his mind!"

"So was Hamlet." Baynes looked at me curiously. "You mean that crack about a 'family resemblance' didn't register? Even though in Hamlet's family his uncle killed his father and Hamlet pretended insanity so he could kill his uncle?"

"What?" I gaped at him. "But—but——"

"Don't you see? *Jack killed Lawford Holmes.*"

Baynes' good humor was restored by my expression. "So you really thought we went there to cure him! Why, that was just a gag so you'd give a good performance. If you'd known the truth, you'd never have been able to hold it back. I wanted to see how much Jack would admit—and he knew it! So he admitted everything. Playing Sherlock Holmes to the hilt, he described himself by legitimate deduction so carefully that a moron couldn't miss it."

"Thanks!" I interjected, but the irony was wasted. Baynes went on.

"Finally, to rub it in, he added that business about Hamlet. To *me* he said that, with a straight face!"

"Then being crazy——?"

Baynes reached out and seized my Bartlett from the shelf.

"Shakespeare said it first. . . . Here we are. *Hamlet*, Act Two, Scene Two. 'Though this be madness, yet there is method in't.' I always thought the line went, 'There's a method in his madness.' . . . You know, after I learned about him acting Sherlock as a boy, I had a funny feeling the whole thing was too pat. But if he had the doctors fooled, who was I to ask questions? I did keep an eye on him, but I couldn't figure out a reason."

"But Jack couldn't have done it! He's been locked up in Glen Rest for more than a year."

Baynes snorted.

"That's what they think at Glen Rest," he retorted. "If he could get into Hilltop by swinging through the trees, he could get out of Glen Rest and back again the same way. Oh, the mechanics are easy enough.

"Last night he learned his uncle had stopped by on the way to Hilltop—maybe saw the car. During the night he stole out of the cottage, climbed a tree, swung over the wall, and was out. The railway goes right up the valley, past Hilltop. He simply swung onto a slow freight, dropped off at Hilltop, made his way to the top, and swung in through the trees by a route he already knew. Since he planned this long ago, he had a gun hidden waiting for him—an unnumbered gun he could easily have smuggled out of the factory, and loaded with a bullet from the defective batch put out during the war.

"He slipped in and caught his uncle by surprise, held the gun on him while he took Lawford's own gun from the desk drawer. Then he handed his uncle the gun he'd brought and invited Lawford to take a shot at him."

"He did *what?*"

"He told us so. He said Lawford must have fired the gun, then thrown it when it didn't go off. How else could Lawford have got it if Jack didn't give it to him? You don't think

Lawford Holmes kept handy a gun loaded with a bum bullet, do you?"

"But the bullet might have fired."

"That was the chance Jack was taking. If the bullet went off, he got killed. If it didn't, he killed Lawford. As I see it, he was gambling that the bullet was as bad as the others that sent a lot of poor devils to their death. It was his way of dealing the cards out even, of letting Fate help judge his uncle.

"The gun jammed. Lawford threw it at him. Jack side-stepped and knocked his uncle out with a solar plexus punch, which leaves no mark. Then he stage-managed the murder to make it look like suicide."

"Leaving the second gun to give him away?"

"It didn't give him away. It was the mark of vengeance accomplished—for his father and for others, his buddies—the artistic touch that made it an execution and not a murder. The job finished, he caught another freight and was back in Glen Rest before daylight."

"And you knew all this when we went there?"

"Not all. I figured out that tree business for myself. But nobody could swing in through the trees at night unless he'd done it before and knew the way. That meant someone familiar with the grounds, somebody who'd climbed the trees. That seemed like a kid—or a kid who had grown up. Jack Holmes was the only one who fitted. As soon as I realized that, I could put most of the rest together. It didn't take any master-mind to figure out the details."

"The other boys on the case didn't figure it out."

"That still doesn't mean I'm a mastermind."

"When are you going to arrest him?"

"Arrest him?" Baynes looked at me pityingly. "In the first place, I can't prove a word of it. In the second, he has an alibi. He was locked up tight in an insane asylum. Do you suppose the asylum people would admit one of their patients could have been running around loose, committing murder? They'd swear on a stack of Bibles it wasn't possible.

"And suppose I *could* prove everything? Jack's legally insane, attested so by three or four doctors. Would they admit they'd been fooled? Jack would just change asylums, that's all."

Baynes reached for his hat.

"You mystery fellows write a lot about the perfect murder, but I bet you never ran across one like this before. As the killer, Jack committed a foolproof murder. Then as the detective, he legitimately deduced himself guilty from a single footprint. We know he did it, why he did it, how he did it— and still we can't do a thing to him. He'll be 'cured' and become a big man some day. Maybe even governor. Wait and see."

Baynes jammed his hat down over his ears and stamped to the door.

"A family resemblance to Hamlet!" he was snorting, as the door closed behind him. "Blast his eyes! A *family* resemblance!"

I append a clipping from the Waterford *Press* of a month later:

GUN COMPANY HEIR
RETURNS TO HOME

John S. Holmes, who has been undergoing treatment for the aftereffects of a war wound, returned to his home at 123 Waverly Street yesterday.

A special meeting of the Board of Directors of the Holmes Gun and Iron Works, founded by Mr. Holmes's father, voted to place him at the head of the firm as president. The office has been vacant since the death of Lawford Holmes, Mr. Holmes's uncle, last month.

Mr. Holmes will enter upon his new duties at once.

The Mystery
of the Three Blind Mice

Forever after, Andy Adams would remember that tremendous, metallic voice screaming for help, bringing him out of a sound sleep with the blankets tangled around him and his heart thudding wildly.

"Help!" the voice shouted, echoing through Andy's bedroom. "Help!"

To Andy, still half asleep, it was like the voice of a giant in the room with him.

"He's shot me!" the voice cried, as Andy struggled to wake

up. "I suspect mice . . ."

Here the voice faltered. Then the unknown speaker tried again, each word seeming to be a terrible effort.

"I suspect mice . . ."

Then the voice gasped into silence, the final word sounding like m-y-y-y-s-s-s-s.

Andy's blindly groping hand found the chain of the bedside lamp. He looked around him at a totally strange room, noting the loud-speaker on the wall from which the voice had come, while his mind asked a crazy question.

How can anyone be shot by mice? he asked himself, trying to recall where he was and how he got there.

Then he remembered. . . .

"It's the only genuine haunted castle in North America," Porterfield Adams said.

His son Andy, almost as tall as he was but beanpole thin, looked around with awed interest. They were in a huge room, with a stone floor, stone walls, and a ceiling made of tremendous old beams. At one end a fire roared in a great fireplace.

Skins of animals covered the floor—zebras, lions, tigers, giraffes. Mounted heads of big game crowded the walls—water buffalo, wart hogs, tigers, lions, mountain goats, leopards and twenty more.

It was a room such as Andy had never dreamed of being in.

Up to nine o'clock that evening, the night before Thanksgiving, life had been perfectly normal. His mother being in Philadelphia with her ill sister, he and his father had been at home alone. They had been playing chess. Andy had won a game, lost a game, and was sure he could checkmate his father when the phone call came.

Porterfield Adams, who was a detective usually specializing in forgery and embezzlement cases and in authenticating old documents, wills and the like, had returned looking rueful.

"We're going on a case, son," he had said. "I tried to say no but got talked down. Pack a bag. We may be there several days."

Going on a case with his father! Andy was so excited he practically threw his pajamas, toothbrush, and extra shirt into a bag. Then had come an hour's drive through the rolling countryside of southern New England, ending at the strangest house Andy had ever seen. It was only two stories high, built like a square U, but it was made of enormous blocks of crude stone, and looked hundreds of years old. At each end was a kind of square tower. And, most surprising of all, it was completely surrounded by a water-filled moat, thirty feet wide, and could be reached only by a drawbridge. It looked just like old castles he had seen pictured in books.

The drawbridge had been lowered for them, and they had driven over the moat and parked in the space between the wings of the U-shaped building. Then a small man in a red coat and tight red trousers named Robin—a butler obviously—had shown them into the great living room.

And now his father was saying that it actually was a castle and haunted at that!

His survey of the room was interrupted. An enormously fat

man with a totally bald head came gliding out of a doorway toward them, riding in an elaborate wheel chair driven by batteries and an electric motor. He came to a stop and, with tiny eyes set in a broad red face, gave Andy and his father a contemptuous stare.

"So you're the detective fella, eh?" he said, in strong English accents. "You don't look like a detective to me. And your name—Porterfield Adams! What sort of name is that for a proper detective?"

Andy felt hot with indignation, but his father remained calm. Taking out his pipe, the sturdily built detective looked at the enormous man in the wheel chair.

"Perhaps you'd like me better if I called myself Sherlock Holmes," he remarked. "And perhaps I'd like you better if you called yourself Sniffy Crumshaw."

For a moment Andy thought the big man would explode. He turned beet red and swelled up like an angry turkey gobbler. Then he let out a guffaw.

"You'll do," he said, as if satisfied. "But did you have to bring your brat with you?" And he turned on Andy a gaze of such intensity that Andy felt his skin crawl.

"My son," Porterfield Adams said, puffing pipe smoke. "You said your problem concerned stamps. Andy is a stamp collector. I brought him along as a consultant."

"Indeed?" And the fat man drawled the word like an insult. "Well, my lad, if you're such a bright lad, perhaps you can tell me what a killer is?"

It was such an unexpected question Andy blinked. But he

thought he knew the answer.

"A killer, sir," he said, "is part of an obliterator."

A smile twitched at his father's lips. The fat man lifted bushy eyebrows.

"Now that may be," he said, "but suppose you tell me when a killer is *not* a part of an obliterator."

"When stamps are canceled," Andy answered, "the obliterator, which is usually known as the cancellation, consists of two parts. One is the postmark. The other part, which actually obliterates the stamp, is called the killer. If a sheet of stamps is canceled just so it can be sold at a reduced price to a collector, without being used for postage, there would be no postmark. Then the killer would be just a killer, I expect."

The fat man's expression did not change. But when he spoke after a long moment in which they could hear the fire crackling and the November wind howling through the branches of the many oak trees around the castle, his voice was civil.

"I am happy," he said, "to meet a fellow collector. Do you specialize?"

"In United States commemoratives," Andy told him.

"I," the fat man said, "specialize in rarities and errors of the most valuable type. I am happy to say that I own at least one, and sometimes as many as six, specimens of every important stamp known."

His lower lip thrust out as he said it, and Andy understood. The man was testing his knowledge.

"Excuse me," he said. "Maybe you are forgetting the one-cent magenta of British Guiana, issue of 1856?"

"What about it?" The huge head lowered as if the man in the wheel chair was about to butt Andy.

"It is so rare that only one copy is known. Scott's catalogue values it at $50,000, but I've read the present owner won't sell. And I do know, sir, that you don't own it. So you can't own *every* important stamp known."

"No, you're right." The man's voice rumbled from deep in his chest. His face purpled again, and he seized a flexible rhinoceros-hide cane which lay on a nearby table and began to whack it furiously on the table top.

"I don't own it! I'll pay anything for it. A million dollars. And the idiot who owns it won't sell it. But I'll own it someday, somehow, or my name isn't Nigel Mayfair!"

And he whacked the table half a dozen times more before he stopped, panting, to glare at Porterfield Adams.

"I know what you're thinking, you detective Johnny," he growled. "You're thinking my name *isn't* Nigel Mayfair. Well, it isn't. But so help me, I shall own that one-cent Guiana stamp sooner or later. And then, sir, then I will be the world's foremost collector of stamp rarities!"

He got his breath and let it out with a roar.

"Henderson! Where are you? I want you!"

A tall, good-humored-appearing man in tweeds walked in from the next room.

"Right here, sir," he said.

"Henderson," Nigel Mayfair grunted, "this is Adams, the detective fella you persuaded me to send for. Adams, Bert Henderson, a solicitor—no, it's lawyer in this country—one of my legal Johnnies."

They shook hands. Then the sandy-haired lawyer shook Andy's hand firmly.

"Glad you could both come," he said. "Do you want to give Mr. Adams the details now, sir?"

"No, blast it, not yet. First I want him to meet the rest of the scavenging jackals who live by picking the flesh from my bones. Where's Pardo?"

"Coming now, sir." A burly man with broad shoulders, dressed expensively, came walking down a flight of carpeted stone stairs from the second floor.

"Pardo!" Nigel Mayfair roared. "This is Adams, the detective. With his help I'm going to put somebody in this house behind bars. That is, if I don't do something worse to 'em."

"Yes, sir," Pardo said; his accent also was English.

"Pardo is my bruiser, my bodyguard and chauffeur," Mr. Mayfair said. "But that doesn't mean he may not be the jackal who has had the nerve to rob me. . . . Pardo! Where's my sister-in-law and that human excuse of a stepson who's been inflicted on me for my sins?"

"They will be down in a moment, sir," Pardo said. His tone was that of a trained servant, but the look he gave Mr. Mayfair was ugly with hate. "They are dressing to go to the party which Mr. Howard Muyskens is giving this evening to celebrate the fact that tomorrow is Thanksgiving. They wish me to drive them. Shall I do so, sir, or shall I call them a taxi?"

"Drive 'em, drive 'em," the fat man roared. "What do I care how they get to the house of that unprincipled thief? The mere fact they defy me and go speaks for itself. Ah, here they are."

He turned his chair, and Andy and his father saw a handsome woman, in evening dress and expensive furs, coming down the stairs. A young man in a tuxedo, his pale face sulky, was at her side. They reached the main floor and paused. Nigel Mayfair glowered at them.

"So you're going," he said. "After I told you I think he's conniving at having me robbed. After I told you he's no better than a thief and a blackguard and a swindler."

The woman shrugged.

"My dear Nigel, you're just ridiculous," she said. "Howard is a fine man. You're merely jealous of him because he has shot specimens of big game larger than you ever did, and is a much better judge of stamps than you."

"Be careful you don't drive me too far, Mollie," Nigel Mayfair growled. "Just because I was married to your sister doesn't allow you to speak to me as you choose."

"This is America," his sister-in-law said. "And you are no longer a petty king ruling over a frightened kingdom. I wasn't going to tell you yet, but I will. I'll be leaving this ridiculous castle for good, soon. Howard Muyskens and I are going to be married."

Nigel Mayfair drew a deep breath. Andy waited for an explosion—but it did not come. In the silence Reggie, the stepson, spoke.

"And I'll go with my aunt," he said. "Tomorrow, however, I have a date to join a sports car rally. Just wanted you to know. Good night, dear stepfather. Pleasant nightmares."

"Tomorrow one of you may be in jail!" the fat man roared.

Without turning they walked out of the room, followed by Pardo, the chauffeur.

"So she's going to marry Muyskens, eh?" Nigel Mayfair growled, half to himself. He looked at the lawyer, Henderson. "Maybe she's the one. Maybe that's her reward for stealing my stamps from me? Or maybe Reggie is doing it for her— he's devoted to her. They both hate me. Just like everybody in this house hates me.

"You hear that?" he demanded of Porterfield Adams. "Everybody who meets me hates me. You'll come to hate me, too, you'll see."

Andy thought his father was going to laugh, the fat man sounded so full of self-pity. But though his lips twitched, the detective's expression never changed.

"I imagine you make it easy for them," he commented.

Nigel Mayfair gave him a sour look.

"No impertinence, my man!" he snapped. "You're just a hired hand here to do a job, so don't get above yourself."

"Andy." His father turned to him. "On second thought I've decided not to take Mr. Mayfair's case, whatever it is. Let's get the car and return home."

"No!" The fat man's roar filled the room. "Confound it, you New Englanders are so touchy. Have been ever since that Boston Tea Party business and that was almost two hundred years ago. Come in to my private study and let's get down to brass tacks. . . . And," he added, as Porterfield Adams hesitated, "I expect you to bill me for the services of your consultant, too."

Andy looked at his father so excitedly that Porterfield Adams gave a reluctant laugh.

Maybe, Andy was thinking, I really will be able to help. Until now, his father's work had always seemed mysterious to him, but if this case involved stamps . . .

"All right," the detective said. "Lead the way."

"Henderson, I'll call you when I need you." The fat man turned the wheel chair, and it rolled toward a doorway. Henderson nodded cheerfully to Andy and his father and settled down on a sofa covered in leopard skin.

"If he starts yelling too much, I'll come in," he half whispered. "Mr. Mayfair sometimes gets a bit—well, excited."

Andy, following his father, found himself in a much smaller room. It too, however, seemed to have walls of crude stone, covered with animal skins. Several suits of armor on stands stood along the floor, and on the walls were just six mounted big game heads—a lion, a tiger, a mountain goat, a black leopard, a water buffalo and a grizzly bear. Andy had seen living animals of these species in zoos, but these heads must have come from specimens that were absolute giants. Even mounted, they seemed tremendously alive, as if about to leap upon them all and rend and tear them to bits.

"Close the door," Nigel Mayfair directed, and Andy did so. The fat man waved his rhinoceros-hide cane toward two chairs, and they sat down. Porterfield Adams was puffing calmly on his pipe, but Andy was almost quivering inside with excitement, though he tried hard to imitate his father and seem calm.

"This cane," said the fat man in the wheel chair, "came from the skin of a rhino I shot myself. Those heads on the wall —shot 'em all myself. They're the largest ever taken, I don't care what that blackguard Howard Muyskens says. If he has larger, he got 'em by a trick—natives trapped 'em or something."

On the point of getting into a fury, he calmed himself.

"Going to talk about myself for a moment," he said. "Want you to understand me. Important to understand the kind of man you're dealing with, eh, detective fella?"

Andy's father nodded. "It helps," he said.

Andy listened, eyes and ears both wide open.

"Well," said Nigel Mayfair, "I'm a collector, see. Started life in a London slum. Not nice. Then or now. Sharpens a lad's wits, though." He bared his teeth in what Andy supposed was a grin.

"That's when I was named Sniffy Crumshaw. Had a cold all the time. Runny nose. Those days I collected bottles. Cleaned 'em and sold 'em for half a cent each. When I got enough money, I went to South Africa. Got a job with a big diamond-mining company. Figured out a brand-new way to smuggle diamonds out of the mines, past the guards. I was a millionaire before I was twenty-one. Then I collected my name. Nigel Mayfair. More aristocratic sounding."

His eyes bored into theirs.

"Yes, sir. When I was Nigel Mayfair, gentleman millionaire, I started collecting money. Collected plenty of it. When a chap collects anything—money or anything else—sometimes he forgets about the nice points of the law, eh?" And he bared his teeth in another sharklike grin.

"When I had enough money, I started collecting big game. Real thrill in those days, shooting big game. Married a British aristocrat—widow of a duke. We had a grand time. But then a tiger killed her in India and I was saddled with her pasty-faced son Reggie and her sister, Mollie Rainier, both of whom you saw. They live off me and look down on me 'cause I was born in a slum and they were born in a manor house.

"Well, I caught a tropical illness. Made an invalid out of me. So I moved here, to New England. Doctor fellas said the climate would do me good. To show Reggie and Mollie what money can do, I went out and bought myself a whole castle —this one. Castle Cragie, it was called. It came complete with ghost, though he doesn't show himself these days—maybe he didn't like crossing the Atlantic."

The fat man's eyes gleamed with satisfaction now, and his voice had become almost a purr.

"Yes, I bought a castle—not big, but real. And old. Stood on the Scotland-England border for four hundred years. Changed hands a dozen times. Blood ran deep on these floors more than once in the days when the Scots and the British were constantly at war."

He said it so happily that Andy glanced down and moved his feet, almost as if expecting to see a pool of blood. His father winked at him, meaning, *Let him enjoy himself talking*. His father had often told him that the more a man talked, the more you could tell about his character, his personality, and even how he would be apt to think.

"So I brought every stone here and had it put up the way it was. Castle Cragie had a drawbridge. I kept the drawbridge and put a real moat around it. Of course I added electricity, an elevator, things like that; but just the same, I'm the only man in North America who lives in a genuine haunted castle with a moat around it. That's a satisfaction, knowing you have something no one else has. Believe me it is, lad." And he spoke now to Andy.

"As a collector, you know how much fun it is to have a rare stamp your friends don't have. Well, I have things no other man has. And now that I'm an invalid, and have to collect stamps, I'm going to have stamps nobody else has! The most, the best, and the rarest!"

And to punctuate his statement, he whacked the rhinoceros-hide cane loudly against the floor.

"I think we understand," Porterfield Adams said now, putting his pipe away. "But that still doesn't tell me—us—anything about your problem." Andy felt a little thrill of pride when his father added that "us."

"So it doesn't. Well, step to the wall." Nigel Mayfair used the whip to point. "Pull back that zebra skin."

The detective rose and did so. Behind the zebra skin, Andy was startled to see a great steel vault with a man-sized square door, the bottom flush with the floor. It seemed to Andy to have a very elaborate combination lock.

"Open it," the fat man growled. "I unlocked it when you came. And snap that light switch beside the door."

Porterfield Adams tugged at the handle and the vault door swung open. Behind it was a strongroom, six feet wide by eight feet long and six feet high. The walls were of steel. In it were a small desk and a chair, and shelving, hung low, which held dozens of large, leather-bound books.

"My treasure chest. I can roll my chair right into it," Nigel Mayfair said. "More'n a million dollars' worth of stamps in there. Fireproof. Burglar proof. Even if an army with cutting torches tried to burn their way in, they'd be sorry." He gave an ugly chuckle. "Poison gas," he said. "It would flood the vault and this room, too.

"What's more," he told the detective, "the combination is a six-letter word nobody on heaven or earth knows but me. Six letters. Not a chance in a million any thief could stumble on the right combo. But"—and he began to pound the rhinoceros-hide cane violently on the floor—"some beggar has got in. Somebody in this house has got into my vault and stole some of my most precious little beauties!"

"Calm yourself, sir!" Andy's father said sharply. "I understand your feelings, but getting excited doesn't help me get the facts."

"No, of course not." With an effort, the enormous man in the wheel chair composed himself. "But you don't understand, detective fella. I mean, they've robbed *me*, Nigel Mayfair! And taken some of my sweetest rare stamps! To steal from a collector is to steal more than money, sir!"

Porterfield Adams waited. After a moment, Mr. Mayfair began again.

"All right," he said. "It's only half a dozen stamps. Maybe

worth twenty, thirty thousand dollars. But somebody in this house stole 'em. Maybe my sister-in-law. Maybe Reggie. Maybe Pardo, maybe Henderson. Maybe Robin. Maybe Frenchy the chef—no, he just lives to cook. Count him out. But somebody in this house. And I think they sold them to that confounded Muyskens, who lives in the house next to me, only house anywhere near. Or if Mollie did it, maybe she made him a present of 'em. For love. Bah!"

He made an ugly sound in his throat and fixed his eyes on Andy.

"I don't go in there to look at my treasures every day," he said. "Sometimes not for weeks. I might not have discovered the theft for a long time—maybe not until the cheeky thief took everything I own! Only, a little while ago, a couple of chaps reported they had some of the new United States Dag Hammarskjöld commemorative four-cent stamps with errors in them—you know what I mean, eh?" he asked Andy.

"Yes, sir." Andy did know. "Several men reported having the Dag Hammarskjöld errors. One, out in the Middle West, had used some for postage. Another one, here in the East, had a complete sheet. He valued it highly."

"He did indeed," Nigel Mayfair said. "But I made him an offer to double any other bid, and I'd have gotten it, too. Then I would have had a complete sheet of the first important error in United States stamps since the discovery of a sheet of twenty-four-cent airmail stamps with the airplane in the center inverted, way back in 1918. And you know what happened?" He raised his voice now to a roar. "You know what happened?"

Andy thought he knew what Mr. Mayfair was leading up to. But the fat man did not wait for any answer.

"That Postmaster General in Washington!" he shouted, his face livid, and the limber hide cane swishing down to smack on the floor with almost every word. "He decided to reprint millions more just like the original errors so everybody could have one. Said stamp collecting wasn't a lottery. Why, the brass-bound nerve of the fella. He robbed me of the chance to have that whole sheet of original errors. Worth a genuine fortune someday! Now, I wouldn't have 'em in the house!

"But"—and he was still roaring at the top of his voice, with the veins in his temples standing out in a way that alarmed Andy—"it made me look at my book of rarities and errors. And I found I'd been robbed. And I began to get mad. I wanted someone's hide. Someone's got to be punished, got to pay, got to suffer——"

He was actually screaming now. But just as Andy's father was about to go to him the door burst open and Pardo rushed in, followed by Henderson, and Robin, who looked white and frightened.

"I'll take over, sir," Pardo said, and seized the fat man. As Mr. Mayfair opened his mouth to roar his anger, Pardo put a small bottle to his lips.

"That will help him, Mr. Adams," Henderson said. "It's for his heart and nerves. This stamp business has really upset him —I mean first the losing out on the Dag Hammarskjöld errors, then finding he'd been robbed."

Nigel Mayfair was returning to normal. He still breathed

heavily, but his face turned from purple back to its normal reddish tinge.

"Thanks, Pardo," he said. "You delivered the lady and dear Reginald to my esteemed neighbor's party, eh?"

"Yes, sir," Pardo said. "It appears to be a large, noisy American type party. Mr. Muyskens will bring them back. I shall work on the car if you do not require me. The carburetor needs adjusting."

"After you get me into bed," Mr. Mayfair said. "I'm going to sit up and write a letter to the President, telling him what I think of the Postmaster General. I'll singe the paper, blast him. Adams!"

"Yes?"

"We'll finish our chat in the morning. Ask Robin for anything you want. Pardo, take me upstairs."

"Yes, sir." The big man stepped to the far wall. He pressed a button. What to Andy had looked like rock proved to be a cunningly painted door, which slid back to reveal a small elevator. Nigel Mayfair guided his electric wheel chair into the elevator without looking back.

"Good night, gentlemen," Pardo said, and closed the door. Then he and Nigel Mayfair were gone.

Once they were out of sight, Andy suddenly realized he had been almost too tense to breathe. Mr. Mayfair's rage had been so violent that the boy felt as if he had been through some kind of storm.

The lawyer, Henderson, stepped across to the open stamp vault, closed it and spun the combination. Then he clicked the switch that controlled the light inside the vault.

"He really was upset!" he remarked. "Going off and leaving his treasure chest open. Please witness I closed and locked it. Believe me, he suspects me as much as anyone else in this ridiculous castle."

He cocked an eyebrow at Andy.

"What do you think of Mr. Nigel Mayfair?" he asked.

"I don't like him!" Andy said. "He practically boasted that all his life he's lied and cheated and stolen to get what he wanted."

"If not much worse," Henderson said.

"At any rate," Porterfield Adams remarked, "things should be quiet now. You can give me a few facts, if you don't mind, Mr. Henderson."

"Glad to."

"And you, son, ought to get to bed now." He smiled at Andy. "I'll be along soon. Nothing much more can happen tonight, I'd say."

He was wrong. Very wrong. But they would not know that for almost an hour.

Robin, the butler, led Andy up the broad stairs to the second floor, to a room a short way down a wide hall. It was a huge room, with furniture that looked very old, and two immense beds with carved bedposts. On one of them lay Andy's pajamas. His father's lay on the other bed.

"Tonight, Master Andrew," the butler said, "you will sleep in a bed in which kings have slept. Not English kings, but kings for all that. Every stick of furniture Mr. Mayfair owns was bought from various European royal households. Where he walks, kings walked. Where he sits, kings sat. He—ah—enjoys the thought."

It gave Andy a queer feeling to think he was going to sleep in a bed that had once been occupied by a king, or maybe kings.

He walked over to the windows and looked out. He could see one wing of the building, looming large and dark at his left. A light on the second floor was on. To his right he could make out the east wing of Castle Cragie. A whole row of lights were on.

The wind was whipping and lashing the oak trees that stood on the grounds beyond the moat, and he could see a positive blaze of lights appearing and disappearing off to his left, just beyond the end of the west wing, but quite a distance away.

"What's that light, Robin?" he asked, not sure how one talked to a butler.

"The light in Mr. Henderson's room, sir. He has the last room in the west wing. Mr. Mayfair occupies the entire east wing himself."

"No, I mean off there in the distance."

"Oh, that. That is Mr. Howard Muyskens' residence, where the party is. Mr. Muyskens and Mr. Mayfair were once friends and indeed, partners, but I fear they are enemies now. Would you like a hot bath, sir?"

Andy decided he would, especially when he saw that the room had a private bath with a tub almost big enough to swim in, made of solid pink marble with real gold fixtures.

"What temperature do you prefer, Master Andrew?" Robin asked, as he turned on the water. Andy had never thought of taking the temperature of a bath. It was either too hot, or too cold, or just right. But he tried to be nonchalant.

"Whatever you think, Robin," he said, and couldn't help feeling a little embarrassed at having a grown man help him take a bath. "Tell me," he asked, as Robin turned on the taps, "did Mr. Mayfair shoot all those animals downstairs?"

"Oh, no, sir." The little man got an immense towel out of a cabinet and folded it for use.

"Miss Rainier, his sister-in-law, shot some. His stepson Reginald shot some. One or two were shot by Pardo, and I have the honor to be represented by a small but rare species of cheetah."

"Then everybody in the house is a big-game hunter?" Andy asked in surprise.

"Everybody but cook, sir. Even Mr. Henderson has done a bit of shooting. Only deer, however."

Andy hoped he wasn't being too nosy, but a detective had to ask questions and get information, didn't he? And he might learn something that would help his father.

"Robin," he asked, "does everybody really hate Mr. Mayfair?"
The butler cleared his throat.

"Mr. Mayfair makes himself easy to dislike, sir," he said.

"Do you hate him? Does Pardo hate him? Everybody?"

"If Mr. Mayfair had not already stated the fact," the little man said with dignity, "I would not speak of it. But it is true.

We all hate him completely. Even Miss Rainier and Mr. Reginald."

"Gosh, then, why do you stay around?" Andy burst out. "This is America, not—not someplace else."

"It is not that simple, Master Andrew. Sometimes one makes —shall we say, a misstep? It is very easy, especially when one is desperate. Mr. Mayfair has certain papers in a small steel box in his vault which keep us loyal and faithful to him."

"You mean he blackmails you?"

"I do not like that word, Master Andrew."

"Even Mr. Henderson?" Andy asked. Robin nodded. "And Miss Rainier? And Reggie?"

"Miss Rainier and Mr. Reginald," Robin said, "are quite penniless and in debt. Mr. Mayfair supports them but will not let them leave. Meanwhile he withholds a small estate his wife left them, which would enable them to be independent. Now, sir, would you care to have me return to towel you when you finish your bath? Or shall I remain to assist in scrubbing your back?"

"Gosh, no!" Andy burst out. "I can bathe myself. Uh— that will be all," he finished, using a line he had heard in a movie.

"Very good, sir. Good night."

Robin seemed to glide out, and Andy gave a little sigh of relief. He didn't think he would like having a servant around all the time.

Still, the bath in the huge tub with the gold fixtures was rather fun, and he prolonged it because he felt sure he would never encounter such luxury again. When he finally tumbled into one of the two big beds, he was asleep almost before he could turn out the light.

And it was out of a sound sleep that the giant voice awakened him, echoing through the room.

"Help!" the voice cried. "Help!"

Andy shot bolt upright in bed, fighting to get loose from the blankets, trying to get his eyes open.

"He's shot me!" the voice screamed, so metallic and distorted that Andy couldn't recognize it. "I suspect mice . . ."

Then the voice faltered before the unknown speaker tried again, this time the words coming slowly, as if with great effort.

"I suspect mice . . ."

The voice gasped into silence, so that the last word was long drawn out, sounding like m-y-y-y-s-s-s-s.

Andy's blindly groping hand found the chain of the bedside lamp. He looked around at the strange room, trying to recall where he was and how he got there.

Then he remembered and leaped out of bed. His father's bed had not been touched. He ran to the door, flung it open and dashed into the hall. Down the hall he saw his father disappear through a door, and he raced after him.

"Dad!" he called. "Dad!"

Apparently his father did not hear him. The door closed. But when Andy reached it, he wrenched it open and darted inside. He found himself in a tremendous room with many windows, hung with rare old tapestries. His father was standing beside a great four-poster bed where Mr. Nigel Mayfair lay slumped on his side, gasping for breath, eyes shut, one hand still beside the button of the communicator into which he had been shouting, and which apparently connected with all the other rooms in the house. The bed reading lamp was on and some papers were scattered on the pillow.

Porterfield Adams turned.

"Andy!" he said. "Someone's shot Mayfair. Sitting up in bed with the light on, he was a perfect target. He may be dying. We have to get a doctor."

He bent over the communicator, which had enabled Mr. Mayfair to speak to all parts of the house.

"Robin! Pardo!" he shouted. "Get here at once!"

Then he straightened. His gaze went to the window. Andy's followed. In the center window, he saw three bullet holes, neat round punctures surrounded by radiating cracks. Drawn by a strange fascination, Andy walked toward the window. He looked out, through one of the bullet holes, and saw again, directly in his line of vision, the lights of the Muyskens residence, blinking and winking at him.

"Dad," he began, turning. But before he could speak, Pardo rushed into the room, his hands black with grease. Behind him came Robin, tugging on his red jacket, and immediately after Robin was Mr. Henderson, still pulling a robe over his pajamas and wearing one bedroom slipper.

Porterfield Adams issued crisp orders.

"Robin!" he said. "Phone Mr. Mayfair's doctor. Tell him to get here at once, and have the nearest hospital send a fully equipped ambulance to meet him. Pardo, do anything you can for Mr. Mayfair. He's still alive, but just barely. Henderson, check the grounds to see if anyone outside could have fired those shots. I'll phone the State Police. . . . Oh, and Andy —go back to bed!"

Andy had been about to tell him he knew where the shots had come from. But when his father used that tone, it was no time for talk.

"Yes, sir," he said and started for his room.

It was only after he was in bed that he realized what kind of mice had tried to kill Mr. Mayfair.

Seriously wounded, Mr. Mayfair had tried to gasp into the house communicator the name of the person he suspected. He had been trying to say, "I suspect Muyskens." Only, he had just been able to get out the *mice* sound.

And then another idea came to Andy. Maybe he had been trying to say, "*My* sister-in-law." That started with the *mice* sound, too. Or even, "*My* stepson." Another *mice*.

Three mice, Andy thought, yawning, and any of them might have shot Mr. Mayfair. His thoughts began to spin in queer circles. . . . *Muyskens . . . my sister-in-law . . . my step-son . . . three mice and we're the blind ones because we don't know which of them did it . . . the mystery of the three blind mice . . .*

Finally, in spite of all the excitement of the evening—or perhaps because of it—he was asleep.

When Andy woke, it was broad daylight. His father's bed had been slept in, but his father was missing. Andy's wrist watch said 9:30. Why, they might have solved the whole case of the stolen stamps and the shooting of Mr. Mayfair already, for all he knew.

He washed, brushed his teeth, slid like an eel into his clothes, and dashed out of the room. In the hall, he paused. Down at the end, the door to Mr. Mayfair's room was open.

Drawn irresistibly, he walked quietly toward it. When he reached it, he saw the room was empty. Mr. Mayfair had been taken away, probably to a hospital. If the door had been closed, he wouldn't have gone in, but as it was wide open, he now walked in boldly.

In the carved wood of the headboard was a bullet hole— apparently one bullet had missed, probably when Mr. Mayfair rolled over to shout for help into the communicator beside the bed.

Someone had taped a black string beside the bullet hole and the string led straight to the window. Eagerly Andy went to the window and saw that the string was taped there just beside the third bullet hole. He could tell it was the third bullet hole quite easily.

The first bullet, cutting a clean hole through the glass, had left cracks radiating out to the edges of the pane. The second bullet had left cracks which stopped when they met the cracks made by the first bullet. The third bullet's cracks stopped even sooner—when they met the cracks made by the second bullet.

Andy could see what the idea was. By lining up the two holes made by the same bullet, someone had been determining the exact line of flight of the bullet!

Andy bent over and sighted along the string. His gaze went

through the hole in the glass and, just as he had expected, it ended directly at the terrace on the side of the large brick and timber house several hundred yards away, and up a slight rise. The home of Mr. Howard Muyskens.

Andy stood and looked over the whole landscape with great care.

The wind of the night before had died down. He could see a section of the thirty-foot moat which surrounded Castle Cragie. The water was glittering in the sunlight. Beyond it was a line of oak trees, spaced evenly apart, then a stone wall, then three hundred yards farther, the Muyskens residence.

And the bullet had come directly between two oak trees, where a space of six feet or more gave a clear view, straight into Mr. Mayfair's room.

In its flight, it had cleared the end of the west wing of Castle Cragie by about five or six feet. Andy transferred his gaze to the west wing, to see if he could be wrong, if by any chance the shot could have been fired from there.

The very end window, in Mr. Henderson's room, was open a few inches, but the angle was all wrong. The shot couldn't have been fired there. Maybe if there was a ledge—but there wasn't any ledge. No, the shot could not have been fired from the house, nor from anywhere on the grounds that he could see—the paved terrace, the green lawn, the little garden below him, between the building and the moat.

Then Andy's heart leaped with excitement. Just beyond the west wing he could see the lower section of a ladder leaning against the building. It obviously leaned against the end of the west wing. He could see easily enough that no one could have stood on top of it to fire the shot, because they would have been around the corner of the building and would not even have been able to see Mr. Mayfair's window. But he had another idea, such a startling idea that he wondered if his father had thought of it. Why, if he was right, it could change the whole picture of the case!

He ran out pell-mell to find his father. Dashing down the stairs, he almost knocked little Robin down.

"Robin," he cried as he steadied the butler, "do you know where my father is?"

"In the west library, sir." Robin pointed. "He's making notes, I believe."

"And has he solved the case yet?"

"I do not believe so." Robin did not seem the least bit unhappy as he said it. "The State Police are here and have questioned us all. However, it is my impression they are totally baffled!"

"Thanks, Robin!" Andy headed for the door the butler had indicated.

But, passing another door that was partly open, he stopped.

Inside, a police officer he knew, Lieutenant Dick Fields of the nearest State Police barracks, was questioning a tall, hook-nosed man with a shock of black hair. That must be Howard Muyskens, he thought.

Andy didn't mean to eavesdrop, but after all, this was a detective case and he was there as an official consultant, wasn't he? Besides, the door was open. He bent over, just beyond the door, and tied and retied his shoelace while he listened.

"Now, Mr. Muyskens"—Lieutenant Fields' voice sounded weary—"here is a rifle which my men fished out of the moat. It is a Belgian hunting rifle, with a telescopic sight, and I imagine it is probably accurate up to 500 yards."

"A thousand yards," Muyskens said cheerfully. "Wonderful sight, that. Makes the target look ten feet away. Yes, it's my rifle. I kept it in my trophy room along with some others. It must have been stolen from there."

"Have you any idea when?"

"Not the foggiest. That room is at the side of the house. Sometimes I don't enter it for days. Could have been stolen last night, or maybe a couple of days ago. Hmm. I suppose whoever used it threw it into the moat because he was afraid to try to return it with my party going on. Someone might have wandered in."

"You didn't, perhaps, slip away from your party and use this gun yourself?" the Lieutenant asked.

"To shoot old Mayfair? Hardly sporting, Lieutenant, to shoot a man sitting up in bed like that. No, I didn't shoot him. I was with my guests all evening, as you have already learned by asking."

"But you are enemies?"

"Wrong. He may hate me, but I rather admire him. He's so incredible. Actually he's angry because I'm going to marry Miss Rainier. In fact, I settled here to be near her."

"And you haven't been buying any of the stamps stolen from him?"

"Stamps he *says* were stolen. The answer is no."

"Thank you." Lieutenant Fields sighed. "Miss Rainier?"

"Yes, Lieutenant?" Andy heard the voice of the handsome woman he had seen leaving the night before.

"Have you anything to add to your statement of last night?"

"Nothing. I did not shoot Nigel. I admit I could have, and I have often been strongly tempted to kill him. But I didn't. I was with the other guests the whole time."

"But you could have shot him at 300 yards with that telescopic hunting rifle?"

"Easily, my dear lieutenant, easily. I'll be glad to demonstrate my ability if you desire."

"That won't be necessary. Now, Mr. Reginald Whitford."

"Aren't we just wasting time, old man," Andy heard Reggie's languid voice say. "I didn't shoot the old boy either. But I could have, and maybe I would have if I'd thought of it. My alibi is the same—I was with the other guests. Now be a good fellow and let me have some breakfast? I have a sports car rally to attend this afternoon."

As it seemed the questioning would be coming to an end, Andy hastily headed for the west library, where he found his father seated at a desk, bending over a sheet of paper.

"Dad!" he said excitedly. "Is Mr. Mayfair . . . well, is he . . .?"

"He's at the hospital, unconscious," his father said, looking up. "It's touch and go. If he lives, it may be days before he can talk."

"And you haven't any idea what mouse shot him?" Andy

blushed, realizing his slip of the tongue, but his father chuckled.

"That *mice* thing has been driving me and the police a bit daffy, too, son," he said. "Oh, here's Lieutenant Fields. Learn anything more, Dick?"

"Not a thing." The youngish, trimly erect State Trooper sat down at the desk. At that moment Robin came in with a tray, which held two cups of coffee, a glass of milk, two soft boiled eggs and a pile of toast. He put the coffee in front of the men and the food before Andy.

"I took the liberty, Master Andrew," he said. Andy, suddenly ravenous, was glad he had. He began to eat as the two men talked.

"We've got to make an arrest fast, Porter," Dick Fields said, sipping his coffee. "Otherwise think of the stories in the papers! A real castle—a moat and a drawbridge—a locked vault—a millionaire stamp collector—a shot out of the night. The victim tries to name the one he suspects and can only say *mice!* Wow! The headlines!"

"That vault." Porterfield Adams' brow wrinkled. "I wish we could get it open. Until we do, we don't know what's been stolen. Also, there might be a clue inside."

"Robin told me Mr. Mayfair keeps papers there that would cause trouble for the people who work for him!" Andy burst in. "He blackmails them into being loyal to him even though they hate him."

"Exactly." Lieutenant Fields nodded. "Not a nice man, Mr. Mayfair. But I don't think that vault will open until he gives us the combination."

"A six-letter word will open it, and only Mayfair knows the right word," Porterfield Adams said, puffing pipe smoke. "We could try a hundred thousand words and never hit the right one. Yet, obviously, in spite of all Mayfair's cleverness, someone in this house guessed or discovered the word. It's up to us to do the same."

"Stamps!" Andy said suddenly. They looked at him. "I mean," he said, swallowing a corner of toast, "it's a six-letter word and it's what he was interested in. Maybe it's the code word."

His father shook his head. "Good try, son," he said, "but we thought of that. Also of Africa, where he made his money, Helena, his former wife's name, Castle and Cragie, and lots of others. No go."

"We'll just have to forget the vault," Lieutenant Fields said. "Anyway, if we can arrest the one who shot him, we'll have the thief, too. Apparently your arrival here last night, Porter, alarmed the thief and made him desperate, so he thought he had to kill Mayfair to foil the investigation."

"I wonder . . ." The detective's brows creased still more. "Maybe the thief planned all along to kill him last night and went ahead anyway in spite of my being here."

"You mean because it was the night of the party?" Andy asked. "It was probably the only chance Miss Rainier and Reggie had to get out of the house. And the confusion of a big party would have given them, or even Mr. Muyskens, lots of opportunity to slip out and shoot Mr. Mayfair without their absence being noticed."

"Exactly." His father looked pleased at his deductions. "It put several suspects on the scene and lots of confusion to cover their tracks. No, Dick, this crime was planned. It wasn't a spur of the moment thing. Now I have a sketch here—it shows the layout of the grounds and the path of the bullet."

Adams pushed a sheet of paper into the middle of the table and Andy and Lieutenant Fields studied it.

The Lieutenant nodded. "Good job," he said. "Certainly does seem to pin the shooting on Muyskens, Reggie or Miss Rainier, doesn't it?"

"Straight as an arrow—only there's no way to choose among our three 'mice.' However——"

"Dad!" Andy was almost squirming with eagerness. "The ladder. You have it in the sketch. There, leaning against the end of the west wing."

"Yes?" His father looked at him questioningly. "What about it?"

"I have an idea!" Andy almost exploded with the word. "Please, can we try it? It's about the ladder!"

"Porter, I think your son is becoming a detective," Lieutenant Fields remarked. "Let's have him show us his idea about the ladder, whatever it is."

"Of course." The detective drained his coffee and clapped Andy on the shoulder. "Let's go, son."

It took only a minute or so for them to let themselves out on the paved terrace behind the main hall of the house. They walked around the corner of the west wing of the building and found a heavy, wooden extension ladder leaning against a second-floor window sill.

"The ladder has been there a week," Porterfield Adams remarked. "A mason started to fix the mortar of the window sill and got sick, so he didn't finish. Now what's your idea?"

"We have to take the ladder down," Andy said. "I wasn't sure it was an extension ladder, but it is—a forty-footer."

"Right. Dick, lend a hand. It'll need us all to get it down."

The ladder was heavy. As they swung it out from the house and balanced it upright, it almost fell. But they caught it and lowered it swiftly. Andy, almost breathless with excitement, pulled the rope that extended the two-part ladder to its full length.

"Now," he said, puffing, "we have to lay it across the moat."

"By George!" Dick Fields looked at him with admiration. "Porter, do you realize neither you nor I ever thought of this ladder being used as a bridge? We thought of other things, but not of a bridge. Your son has shown us we aren't as smart as we thought we were!"

"He certainly has," Porterfield Adams agreed. And as the three of them eased the ladder out, until it lay across the thirty-foot moat, with plenty to spare, he asked, "What made you think of it, son?"

"I saw a ladder in a newsreel used as a bridge to rescue a woman from a burning house," Andy said. "I remembered it. Now look."

He ran lightly across the moat and back, leaping from rung to rung of the ladder in rubber-soled shoes with goatlike agility.

"See?" he cried. "The guilty man doesn't have to be just one of the three who were at the party. Anybody in the house could have got across the moat, sneaked up to steal the rifle, shot Mr. Mayfair, come back, dropped the rifle in the moat, put the ladder back—and pretended to be innocent."

"There's a whole bunch of new headaches for you, Dick," Porterfield Adams chuckled. "New suspects, everything."

"Let's put the ladder back," Lieutenant Fields suggested. "Now, Andy," he said, as they struggled to get the ladder back into position, "the danger with making deductions is that you are apt to make a good one, then stop. It's easy to be so pleased with yourself that you don't look for flaws or further possibilities."

They lowered the ladder with a thump against the window sill and the Trooper dusted his hands.

"Your idea is a good one, a very good one. But take it farther. We three just had a bit of trouble getting that ladder down and up, didn't we?"

"Yes, sir." And Andy suddenly felt crestfallen. How could he have overlooked something so obvious? "You mean, even though one man could handle a ladder like this, it would take him a long time, especially at night? Much too long for anybody in this house to try, especially since Dad and I saw Robin and Prado and Mr. Henderson all upstairs just two or three minutes after the shooting?"

"That's it, boy," Lieutenant Fields nodded. Then Andy had another idea. They seemed to be coming to him quick and fast today. Once he started trying to be a detective, it seemed as if he couldn't turn off his mental machinery.

"Suppose they were all in it together?" he said. "All three of them! Then they could have got the ladder down and up fast, and any of them could have done the shooting—they all know how to handle rifles."

"Wow!" Lieutenant Fields exclaimed. "Porter, another idea we overlooked! If this boy were a few years older, I'd march him back and enroll him in State Troopers school. Even if his ideas aren't right, they're interesting!"

"Well?" Andy scowled, a little belligerent now. "Why isn't that a possible idea?"

"It is a possible idea, Andy," his father said. "And a mighty good one. It could have been worked. But don't forget, Mr. Mayfair suspected someone. He probably had good reason for that suspicion. And he tried to tell us who it was. That was the whole point of the *mice* message he couldn't finish."

For a moment that subdued Andy. Then, being much too worked up with the excitement of detection to be subdued long, he posed a final problem for the two men.

"Maybe," he said, "Mr. Mayfair was trying to say, 'I suspect *my staff*,' meaning Pardo and Sparrow and perhaps Mr. Henderson, too. That would come out *mice*."

Lieutenant Fields started coughing suddenly. Porterfield Adams nodded.

"Son," he said, "if you were the attorney for the defense we might not be able to convict anyone. But there's still another reason why your idea, though it's ingenious, wouldn't work. At least not under last night's circumstances. Can you figure out why?"

Andy thought for a moment. He remembered the darkness, the way the lights had appeared and disappeared as the oak trees were bent over by the wind, and he thought he knew what his father meant.

"You mean, Dad," he said, "that it was easy for me to run across the ladder just now in daylight, but at night with a wind blowing a man wouldn't be able to run like that? He'd be apt to step between the rungs and break a leg or fall into the water. He would have to get down and crawl across, and that would take much too long—even if all three of them were in on it. They couldn't possibly have arrived at Mr. Mayfair's room so soon after you called."

"That's it." His father seemed very pleased. "You're catching on to the art of being a detective fast. In half an hour we're all going to meet in Mr. Mayfair's bedroom, and Lieutenant Fields and I will try to make someone confess. I'm going to let you be there to watch."

Andy Adams stood pressed against the wall of Mr. Nigel Mayfair's bedroom.

The room, big as it was, seemed rather crowded. His father was there, standing by the bullet-riddled window. Lieutenant Fields stood beside the locked door to the hall. Pardo, Robin and a fat man in a white chef's costume stood ranged on the other side of the bed, looking defiant or frightened. Mr. Henderson leaned against the wall beside Andy, smoking and looking intent. Miss Rainier, the only woman, sat regally at ease in a chair near Porterfield Adams. Reggie, the stepson, lounged in another chair with his legs thrust out in front of him and his hands jammed in his pockets.

"Now, folks," Lieutenant Fields said, "this is an official part of the investigation into the shooting of Mr. Mayfair. Mr. Adams is giving us the benefit of some of his ideas, based on the fact he was here before the crime was committed. Any questions?"

No one had any. Reggie stirred, as if about to say something, then subsided. Porterfield Adams lifted his hand.

"To begin with," he said, "please notice the string between bed and window. This establishes the line of flight of the shots fired at Mr. Mayfair, two of which hit him. Mr. Muyskens, would you like to sight along the string?"

"Gladly." The tall man with the shock of black hair stepped forward, sighted for a long minute along the string.

"The line of flight," he said, "goes exactly between two oak trees and ends precisely on the terrace of my home, three hundred yards away."

"Do you have any comment to make about that fact?"

"I do." Muyskens half smiled. "I can only say that it is a brilliant piece of work."

"Meaning what?"

"Anything you choose." Muyskens smiled and returned to his place.

"Miss Rainier." Porterfield Adams turned to the woman. "Do you care to comment?"

She smiled slightly.

"I can only repeat what Howard said—it's a brilliant piece of work."

"And you, Reggie?" Porterfield Adams asked, turning to the younger man. "Any comment?"

Reggie did not bother to stand. He merely smiled, one-sidedly.

"You're not going to get any help from me," he said. "The old boy's dying, and he deserves it. He terrorized us all. You can't prove a thing on me or Howard or Auntie—we were all at the party and all had equal opportunity to fire that shot. Anyway"—and now, to Andy's amazement, he actually grinned—"the whole thing is a pack of nonsense if only you were smart enough to know it."

"An interesting viewpoint," Andy's father said. "You all know about Mr. Mayfair's last words, which sounded like 'I suspect mice—' and by which he might have meant *Muys*kens, or *my* sister-in-law, or *my* stepson."

He gave each of them a look, and each returned the look with composure. Andy felt his heart beating anxiously. There was no way his father could possibly pick one of the three as guilty. None whatever.

"You all had motives," the detective went on. "You, Mr. Muyskens, perhaps to protect the woman you are engaged to. You, Miss Rainier, if you had been stealing his stamps, to prevent his revealing your theft and having you jailed. You, Reggie, the same motive."

"Motive?" the young man sneered. "I had a dozen motives, Mr. Detective. And I'm only sorry I never could guess the word that opens his precious vault. I'd have left long ago and taken his pretty stamps with me."

"However," Porterfield Adams said now, looking briefly at Andy, "I believe I can almost conclusively prove that all three of you are—innocent."

He waited until the buzz of excited exclamation died down, then continued.

"As for how I know," he said, "Old Mother West Wind told me."

He winked at Andy, to whom, when Andy was small, he had read the famous Thornton Burgess stories. And suddenly Andy understood. How could he have been so blind to such an obvious fact?

"That's meant for a little joke," the detective added. "Actually, however, last night a strong west wind was blowing. It tossed the trees badly. When I looked out this window after Mr. Mayfair's shooting, I saw the lights of your house, Mr. Muyskens, appearing and disappearing. The wind was blowing the oak trees beyond the moat so that half the time, or more, they hid this window from sight from your terrace. Tell me, would any marksman hope to hit a man-sized target at three hundred yards in a high wind, with an oak tree still full of dead leaves blowing back and forth across his line of sight?"

"Of course not," Muyskens said. "I wondered if you'd ever think of that. First place, he couldn't estimate the effect of the wind. Second, the waving branches and leaves would distract his sight. Third, there was a good chance the bullets would be deflected by the tree. No, nobody could have shot old

Mayfair from my terrace last night."

"Well!" There was actually a look of grudging respect on Reggie's face. "You detective fellows aren't as stupid as I thought."

"Wait a minute." Pardo, the chauffeur and bodyguard, strode forward and sighted along the string attached to the window. "If the shot didn't come from there—it couldn't come from any place. Because it certainly couldn't have come from a window in this house. It would have to come out of thin air!"

"In a manner of speaking," the detective agreed. "And when I realized that, I also realized something else. All of you, please stay well back from the bed. What you are about to see is a demonstration, a reënactment of what happened last night."

He threw up the window and made sure they were all well back. Then he adjusted a fat white pillow on the bed and waved his handkerchief out the window. A moment later Andy saw one of the most unexpected sights of his life.

They were all looking out the windows which adjoined the one the bullets had come through. Now they all exclaimed together as they saw, from just around the corner of the west wing of the building, a ladder appear.

It was the same ladder Andy had seen earlier. Now it was moving out into their sight because it was leaning *away* from the building. And a man straddled the top of it, bracing himself. A man in a State Trooper's uniform. A man who carried a rifle.

Andy expected the ladder to crash. But it didn't. Looking closer, he could see a cord running from the top rung back to the end window of the west wing. The ladder leaned about a dozen feet away from the house—and stopped there, held in position by the cord, which must have been tied to something inside the window.

But who had ever heard—who would ever think—of a ladder leaning *away* from a house. Leaning, you could say, against empty air?

Now the State Trooper on top of the ladder braced himself, holding his position with his legs against the rungs. He raised the rifle to his shoulder. He fired. There was a sharp explosion and feathers flew up in a little geyser on the bed in the room. The bullet had hit exactly where Nigel Mayfair, the night before, had been sitting, reading.

No one bothered to watch the State Trooper descend from the ladder, after which someone inside pulled the ladder back against the house. They were all staring at Porterfield Adams.

"So you see," he said, "how a shot could come from nowhere —out of thin air—and *seem* to have come from somewhere. From your terrace," he added, for Mr. Muyskens' benefit. "But since I knew it almost certainly couldn't have come from your terrace, I tried to read the riddle of the bullet from nowhere. And finally it came to me that the top of that ladder, if it swung away from the house, would neatly come across the bullet's line of flight. And from such a short distance, even in a wind, anyone who knew anything at all about a rifle couldn't miss."

"But that means——" Pardo began. And suddenly they were all looking at Mr. Henderson, who stood close beside Andy, leaning against a door.

"Yes, Mr. Henderson." Porterfield Adams' tone was grim. "That hall window the ladder leans against is just outside your room. In your room is a long electrical extension cord—and those cords are very strong—which shows signs of having been tied around something hot—such as the hot radiator just inside the window. By means of its support you were able to push yourself, on the ladder, away from the window, and remain there, perched, as it were, in midair, to shoot Mr. Mayfair.

"No one else could have done the deed in the three minutes that elapsed between the time of the shooting and your appearance. But all you had to do was toss the rifle down into the moat, pull the ladder back against the window, clamber in, and run down the hall to join us. Besides, if anyone else had done it, you would surely have heard the shots and so informed us."

"But he's not a mouse!" It was Andy who spoke. "Dad, he's not a mouse!" Then, blushing crimson, he clamped his mouth shut.

"You mean, son," the detective said, "that his name doesn't begin with s. But Mr. Mayfair is British. And the British call their lawyers 'solicitors.' You heard him call Henderson a solicitor. That's where your 'mice' came from. Mr. Mayfair was trying to say, 'I suspect *my* solicitor'."

Andy gulped. It was true—the wind, the oak tree still full of dead leaves, and the word solicitor—even the ladder, when they held it straight up ten feet from the west wing. He had seen or heard every single clue and failed miserably to deduce the meaning of them. He would never be a detective!

He was startled when Henderson put a strong arm around him. At the same time he felt something hard poking him in the back.

"Alas," Mr. Henderson said. "To be betrayed by a gust of wind. And I thought it was really a very clever plot, too. Or I wouldn't have urged Mayfair to send for you, Adams. But I thought you'd be a little, stoop-shouldered fellow half blind from studying dusty papers, and by actually suggesting you, I persuaded Mayfair he was wrong in suspecting me. That gave me the time I needed to fix up my plan to kill him. Well, under the circumstances, I think it is time for me to say good-by now."

And to Andy's amazement, the door behind them opened. Before any of the others could move, the lawyer dragged him back through it and slammed it shut, and they were in an elevator dropping rapidly downward!

"Mayfair's private elevator," Henderson said. "Don't struggle, boy. I have a gun and I'll use it. Keep calm and you won't be hurt."

The elevator stopped smoothly. The door opened. Henderson shoved Andy out and, still holding him tightly, pulled him across the room so he could lock the heavy door leading into the room.

"The only entrance to the room, and solid oak. It gives us a good five minutes." He grabbed Andy's wrist and twisted it up behind his back. "Over here against the wall, boy, and stand quiet if you don't want a broken arm."

Andy obeyed. Facing away from the wall, he could guess that the man was turning the combination dial of the big vault. He was right, for a moment later it swung open and the lawyer, after clicking on the light inside, marched him in. He sat Andy down in the soft chair that stood behind a desk, and shoved the desk tight against him, pinning him in place.

"Now, my boy," Henderson said, "if you move I have plenty of time to shoot you. If you don't move you have a sporting chance."

He showed Andy the automatic he held, then dropped it into his pocket. Keeping an eye on Andy, he reached for several of the leather-bound loose-leaf stamp albums on the low shelf. Andy did not move. He knew that long before he could get out from behind the desk, the lawyer would have the gun out. Breathing fast, he watched.

"It was a mistake, stealing those first few stamps," the lawyer commented. "But I needed expense money. Now I'll do the job as I planned it all along."

The tall man, humming a little tune, went swiftly through the loose-leaf albums, ripping out plastic strips in which rare and valuable stamps were carefully preserved, and putting them in an envelope. This he put in his pocket. The whole thing hadn't taken a minute.

"There," he said. "Their catalogue value is at least three hundred thousand dollars. I can get a hundred thousand for them in Europe. Well, I must be going. Sorry, but I'm going to have to leave you alone here. Oh, one last job."

He took a small steel box from a shelf.

"This holds Mayfair's evidence against me and the rest," he said. "Everybody will be happy to know I shall burn it."

"You can't get away," Andy said, trying to keep his voice steady. "Listen! They're chopping at the door now."

"So they are. Well, it's worth a try. You see, Andy, I'm going to lock you in here. There's about air enough for five or six hours and no one can possibly unravel the combination in that time. If they agree to give me four hours' head start, I'll telephone your father the combination. Otherwise . . . well, when they get you out, you'll have lost interest in things."

He moved to the vault door and paused, even though outside the vault Andy could hear the sound of an ax being used on the oak door into the room.

"I like you, boy," he said. "I admire your father even though he unmasked me. I was amused by his mention of Old Mother West Wind. So as a sporting gesture I'm going to give you a clue how to figure out the code word to open this vault. Not how I figured it out—for me that was a flash of inspiration— but a clue you can puzzle out while you're waiting. Now listen carefully. I assume you studied some poetry in school. There is a poem called *The Vision of Sir Launfal* written by the poet James Russell Lowell. In it he has one very famous line every school child should know about what makes a June day so perfect.

"Now, I hope you can remember that line, because I'm going to give you a puzzle. Imagine that in the very middle of that June day you are having a picnic, and the menu consists of sausage patties, toasted marshmallows, artichoke heart, mustard pickles and prune whip. If you can solve the puzzle, you'll have a clue to the word which opens this vault. You'll still have to use the clue to figure out the word, so you'll have your work cut out for you. Try thinking about it both forward and backward. And inside out and upside down, if necessary. If that seems bewildering, I can't make it easy, you know, because I do want to get a long way off and hide. If old Mayfair lives, he'll stop at nothing to have revenge on me."

With that he slammed shut the heavy vault door and Andy heard the combination lock turn.

He was alone, in an airtight vault where—if his father couldn't get him out—he would suffocate in a few hours.

Andy shoved the desk away and sprang at the inside of the vault door. He grabbed the handle and twisted it with all his might, in rising panic. His heart was pounding and he seemed unable to get his breath. He couldn't breathe. He was suffocating already!

Then he got hold of himself. He forced himself to be calm. There was air in the vault for several hours, especially if he remained quiet. In that time his father would somehow get the vault open. He was sure of it.

He refused to admit to himself that he wasn't really sure of it at all, but walked over to the desk and sat down. On the desk were the stamp albums Mr. Henderson had looted of their rarities. He scarcely saw them. He was trying to remember exactly what Mr. Henderson had said, and figure out what he had meant by the puzzle he had left as clue to the word that opened the vault.

A line of poetry about a day in June . . . Something tugged at his memory. He had a vision of himself, memorizing a poem in English class. Not a poem—just a few lines. Something about June . . . Then he had it.

And what is so rare as a day in June?

That was all he could remember. It seemed to mean absolutely nothing. Still, puzzles did seem meaningless until you figured them out. And the solution of this one might save his life.

So he wrote down the line of the poem and then under it the crazy menu Mr. Henderson had specified for the picnic.

And what is so rare as a day in June?

MENU

sausage patties
toasted marshmallows
artichoke heart
mustard pickles
prune whip

He stared at it. It meant nothing as far as he could see. None of the words even had six letters! And it wasn't June and this wasn't a picnic. This was Thanksgiving Day, and he and his father should have been at home, roasting the turkey they were going to cook themselves, since his mother was away. Suddenly tears filled his eyes. He couldn't stop them. He didn't try.

Until, unexpectedly, he heard his father's voice.

"Andy! Andy, can you hear me?"

He looked wildly around. But the vault had not opened. The voice was coming from a small round grillwork over the desk. A loud-speaker, such as Mr. Mayfair had all over the house for calling his staff.

"Andy, if you hear me, press the red button under the loud-speaker and answer. Then let go to hear me."

Eagerly Andy pushed the red button.

"Yes, Dad, I hear you."

"Thank heaven for that! Listen, son—we've made a bargain with Henderson. He's to get four hours' head start, then he's to phone me the combination. Do you understand? You'll be all right if you can just keep calm for four hours. The air will last that long, anyway."

"I'll be all right, Dad." Andy said it as firmly as he could.

"We'll be trying to find the combination meanwhile."

"Dad!" Andy interrupted. He told about the clue Henderson had given him, the line of poetry and the picnic with the weird menu. There was a long silence; then his father answered, sounding doubtful.

"That doesn't mean anything I can see," he said. "But we'll get a code expert from the State Police here to work on that angle.

"Meanwhile, stay calm and quiet. We'll be at work and I'll speak to you every few minutes. We can't try to burn open the vault door—you know the reason, don't you?"

"Yes, Dad. I heard Mr. Mayfair say that would flood

everything with poison gas."

"Right, son. Maybe you can kill time by looking at the stamp collection. Just don't get impatient."

That was easy to say, but hard to do. Andy looked at the solid steel walls of the vault all around him, and in his imagination they began to move slowly together as if to crush him. The air seemed to be choking him. His heart pounded, he felt sweat on his forehead. Suddenly he jumped up in a panic and jammed at the red button.

"Dad! Dad!"

"Yes, son?"

He'd been about to ask, *Suppose Mr. Henderson doesn't phone the combination?* But he knew the answer to that. No need to let his father know he was feeling panicky.

"I just wanted to hear your voice."

"Right, Andy. Miss Rainier and Reggie are trying to help us think of words that Mayfair might have used for the combination."

"That's good."

Privately, Andy was sure they would never find it. The fat man had kept the secret word in his head and no place else. Yet, if Mr. Henderson had been able to guess it—well, that proved it could be done. But how could a poem help?

And what is so rare as a day in June . . . sausage patties, toasted marshmallows, artichoke heart, mustard pickles, prune whip . . .

The words seemed to sing in Andy's tired brain, mocking him. They meant nothing, nothing. Why none of them was even six letters long!

To be doing something, he picked up the nearest red-leather bound loose-leaf stamp album Henderson had thrown down. Outside, in gold, was stamped in large, proud letters:

Rarities and Errors
Collection of
Mr. Nigel Mayfair

Andy opened it. The first page he came to was headed:

British Guiana
One Cent Magenta
Issue of 1856

Below that was a space for the stamp in a plastic envelope, and at the bottom was neatly printed a complete history of the world's rarest stamp, beginning with its finding by a boy named Vaughan, who had sold it for a dollar and a half. Now, as the only existing specimen of the stamp, it was worth at least $50,000.

But obviously Mr. Mayfair had never owned it. The stamp belonged to someone else, and that someone else wouldn't part with it. Just the same, the page indicated that Mr. Mayfair had been determined to own the British Guiana one cent magenta—someday, somehow.

Andy turned to the next pages. They were almost all empty. There were pages which had held the Cape of Good Hope triangular errors, the five important rarities from the island of Mauritius, the rare and coveted U.S. Postmaster Provisionals, the blocks-of-four of the tremendously valuable United States airmail invert error of 1918, a complete collection of the very rare Postmaster Provisional issues of the Confederate States in 1861, and scores more. Mr. Henderson had taken them all.

Wishing he could have seen these rare stamps that were beyond the reach of any but the wealthiest collectors, Andy picked a book from the shelf and made himself look through it. It did help to make him forget that the minutes were ticking away, and with every one that passed there was less air left in the vault for him to breathe.

The book he had selected held a complete collection of United States commemorative stamps in blocks of four. Ordinarily Andy would have been interested, but now he couldn't study them long. He pushed the book aside, remembering the rage with which Mr. Mayfair had shouted against the Postmaster General for reprinting the new Dag Hammarskjöld four-cent error so that it wasn't a rarity any more.

As he pushed the book away, his gaze fell on the sheet where he had written down the line of poetry and the fantastic menu. And—perhaps because he had just been thinking about rare stamps—he suddenly noticed that exactly in the middle of the line was the word *rare*. And Mr. Henderson had said, "In the very middle of that June day." Suddenly the first letter in each line of the menu seemed to leap out at him to spell a word:

And what is so *RARE* as a day in June?

MENU

Sausage patties
Toasted marshmallows
Artichoke heart
Mustard pickles
Prune whip

And at that instant he was sure he knew the word, the one word, that Mr. Mayfair could never have forgotten, must always have been thinking of, and had undoubtedly used as the combination to lock his vault!

Andy punched the red button so hard he hurt his thumb. "Dad! Dad!" Excitedly he told his father his deduction.

"Good boy! We'll try it. Now don't be disappointed if it doesn't work."

Andy waited, holding his breath. He had to be right. He just had to! But the vault wasn't opening. By now it should have opened. He was wrong! He jabbed at the red button.

"Dad!" he cried. "What's the matter?"

"Sorry, son." His father's voice was carefully controlled. "Your word doesn't seem to work."

Andy held back an impulse to sob. Now suddenly he couldn't get his breath. The air was all gone. He was suffocating!

For an instant Andy almost flung himself at the huge metal

door and pounded on it with his fists, as if he could open it that way. The only thing that stopped him was his father's voice—not his actual voice now, but the memory of a time when his father had said, "Always remember, son, the tighter the spot you're in, the more important it is to keep calm and not panic."

Breathing hard, he clenched his fists and tried to think. Mr. Henderson had said something else. What was it? Something about how to think about the puzzle he had given Andy for a clue. What had he said? . . . *Think about it forward, and backward, and inside out and upside down, if necessary.*

"Yes!" Andy shouted out loud. "Backward!"

And he punched the red button again.

"Dad!" he called. "Dad!"

"Yes, son?"

"Dad, try the word I gave you again, but this time spell it backwards!"

"Backwards? But . . . well, all right, we'll try it."

Andy could feel his heart beating like a clock, counting off the seconds while he waited. The clock seemed to be getting louder and louder and faster and faster until——

Slowly the vault door swung open and Andy, like a shot, was out and into his father's firm grip.

"Dad!" he said. "Dad! I was scared I was wrong!"

"So was I," his father said. Then, over his shoulder, "Dick, you can start the chase after Henderson now. He's only had half an hour's head start."

"My men are already phoning to have the roadblocks set up,"

came the lieutenant's voice. "Why don't you and Andy go in the library where you can talk?"

In the big library, Andy's father put an arm around his shoulders.

"Son," he said, "you did what a real detective does. You read Mayfair's character, and in that way answered a riddle none of the rest of us could. Now—would you care to tell me how you did it? How you finally hit on the word that opened the vault?"

Andy managed a grin.

"Well, Dad——" and he began to feel pleased with himself again as he told how he had found the clue words, *rare stamp,* in the puzzle Mr. Henderson had propounded for him.

"And Mr. Mayfair wanted to be first in everything," Andy concluded. "He wanted to own things no one else did. Like the only genuine castle in America, and the only private moat."

"That's right."

"But there's one stamp so rare there's only one copy of it in the world—a British Guiana stamp. Mr. Mayfair didn't own it. So with Mr. Henderson's clue, I could just imagine Mr. Mayfair brooding all the time about that rare stamp he didn't own and couldn't buy. It would be on his mind constantly. And it was a six-letter word—G-u-i-a-n-a. I decided that it just had to be the word that opened the vault."

"And it was. Even though it had to be spelled backwards."

"Because Mr. Mayfair had a very twisty kind of mind, Dad. Spelling a word backwards is just the sort of thing he would do. Mr. Henderson gave me a clue to see that, too."

"All the same, Andrew"—Porterfield Adams only used his

son's full name when he was especially proud of him—"you did a fine job of making use of the help Henderson gave you. And one of these days I'd kind of like to be able to change the name of my firm to Adams and Son. How would you feel about it?"

"I'd like it," Andy said.

About the Stories
in this Book

Often I am asked, "How do you get your story ideas?" This can be a very difficult question to answer. A writer does not always know where his ideas come from. They come from life, from things he has seen or heard, things he has read—from many different places. Sometimes ideas form in a writer's mind without his really being aware of them, until suddenly they are there, demanding to be used.

But because the stories in this book are mystery stories, and mystery stories generally revolve around one or two very strong and specific ideas, I can tell you fairly well how I came to write each of them. At least I can tell you how I got started.

Take "Midnight Visitor," for instance. One day I was walking down a street in New York City when I saw an old house from which a fire escape had been removed. Across the front of the house were the marks of the fire escape, but the metal structure itself was gone. I dare say a new one was to be installed.

The idea flashed into my mind, "Suppose in the darkness someone who didn't know the fire escape had been removed tried to use it?" And in that moment the story was born. When I came to write it, I changed the fire escape to a balcony, and then to make it more dramatic I made it a balcony that wasn't really there and had never been there, but that someone was made to *think* was there. So he tried to step out on it and——
Well, you know what happened because I'm sure you've read the story. In any case, the whole idea evolved from my chancing to see that missing fire escape.

The story "Hard Case" came from a newspaper article I read, which told of a hunter who got some mud in the muzzle of his shotgun, so that the barrel exploded when he fired it. Thinking about this, I realized that a shotgun barrel would just hide a roll of money tucked into it. It would certainly be an unusual hiding place, one no one would suspect. But if someone tried to fire the gun——

Well, as you saw when reading the story, I had to add a man trying to trap a criminal into making an attempt to kill him. But essentially the story was born from that newspaper clipping. There are always many details to be added, and things to be changed around, as in a jigsaw puzzle. The important thing to a writer, at least to my kind of writer, is to have the starting idea for making a beginning.

The other stories in this book are more complicated than these two. It would probably take a book in itself to explain all the things I did to them, adding and rearranging, in the course of writing them. But I'll explain how I got started on them. If you are interested in writing, you can go over the stories and note all the things I did, all the things every writer does, when making an idea into a story. The idea is really just the kernel from which the story grows.

The basic idea for "The Blow From Heaven" came in my high school physics class, where I learned that hard iron placed in a magnetic field becomes a permanent magnet. It was many years later that the idea began to grow, and the hard iron became a knife, the magnetic field an electromagnet in the ceiling that held the knife suspended where it would not be noticed. The idea might have been used in other ways, but that is how it came to me.

"Larceny and Old Lace" is a story that I more or less deliberately "thought up." The notion came to me that having a mystery story reader try to solve a mystery by using the ideas learned from mystery novels would be amusing. Gradually the reader became two little old ladies, because the contrast of two little old ladies pitted against tough criminals and winning out seemed funny.

When I had added the idea of some documents hidden in plain sight, after the manner of Edgar Allan Poe's "The

Purloined Letter," I was ready to start writing. "Larceny and Old Lace," for whose title I am indebted to Mr. Ellery Queen, who first published it in his magazine, has been quite a favorite with readers.

One winter when I was a boy I saw some clothes that had been hung out to dry in freezing weather. They had become as stiff as boards. Many years later I saw children sliding down a hill in aluminum bowls, in which they shot along at dizzying speeds. I noticed that in one place, going over hard snow, they left no mark.

This spurred the hidden machinery in every writer's brain, which works even when he doesn't know it. Soon I was thinking about a kind of sled or toboggan made out of a sheet by freezing it stiff, and using it to slide across snow a man couldn't walk on. I saw the possibilities of a seemingly miraculous disappearance, and so "The Glass Bridge" was born. This is a kind of story which mystery writers call an "impossible murder story" and is a favorite type with many. It makes for a great deal of mystification of the reader.

In this case, the explanation went all the way back to a boyhood experience of seeing some wash frozen on the clothesline.

Sometimes the fate of a character hangs by a hair, to use an old familiar saying. In the case of "The Vanishing Passenger" the story itself literally hangs by a hair.

One day it occurred to me that a man could vanish from a speeding train by disguising himself as a woman. But how could the deception be deduced by the detective? I pondered this for awhile, then realized the man would have to wear a wig. And in a wig the individual strands of hair are glued to the foundation material. Real hair is attached to the scalp by a root. Eureka! I thought. A detective finds a long hair. He suspects the presence of a woman. But he finds glue on the end of it, not a natural root. Thus he deduces a wig, and knows that an impersonation is being carried out.

And so "The Vanishing Passenger" began.

"Mr. Manning's Money Tree" was a story that had to be built up bit by bit from a very general idea. I started by wondering how a man, confronted by the problem of hiding some money in a hurry so that he could find it years later, would solve his dilemma.

To make things difficult, I had the man be downtown in a big city, with only a few minutes in which to hide the money. Obviously he couldn't check it at a checkroom. He might have rented a safe deposit box—except that my plan was for him to go to jail, where he couldn't keep up the payments.

Where, then, could he hide it?

I had a house in the country in those days, and one morning I was planting some small trees. Then inspiration came to me. My character could take a bus to the suburbs and find a chance to hide his money under a newly planted tree.

That was just fine. The tree would grow, and when he came back years later it would be quite sizable, very difficult to dig up to get his hidden money. This gave me what every story needs—a difficulty for the chief character to surmount—so I set to work. Little by little the pieces fell into place until finally I had "Mr. Manning's Money Tree."

One autumn day I saw a gray, weatherbeaten, gloomy house in the hills—the kind of house that makes you think instinctively of violence. "That's the kind of house where a murder should be committed," I thought at the time. Later, thinking about it, I decided to write about a house where murder had been committed not once, but twice.

To give the story a surprising and ironic twist, I decided to have the second murderer caught because of the first one's crime.

This was a fine idea, but how could I connect the two crimes? The problem stumped me for some time. Then one day, moving to a new address, I filled out a change-of-address card at the post office. It flashed across my mind that a man who had secretly rid himself of his wife and moved away would have to keep getting her mail in order to avoid suspicion. So he would have to put in the same change of address for her as for himself, whereas if she had actually moved away herself to some other place, she would put in her own change of address.

Again two ideas clicked together and I had a story. After that "Change of Address" was quite easy to write.

Both "The Mystery of the Three Blind Mice" and "The Adventure of the Single Footprint" are rather complicated stories, and it would take a great many words to explain how I developed them. However, I can give you the basic ideas behind them.

In the case of "The Mystery of the Three Blind Mice" the

initial idea came one day when I saw a painter moving a ladder. For a few minutes it leaned away from the house, held by a rope. Instantly the thought occurred to me that someone could climb the ladder and see into a window he couldn't see into with the ladder in its normal position. Or— as I am a mystery writer—it occurred to me he could fire a shot into a window he couldn't otherwise reach. Then if the ladder was put back into place, no one would even think about the possibility of a ladder leaning *away* from a house.

This is the basic idea underlying "The Mystery of the Three Blind Mice" and all the other details were added bit by bit as the story grew.

The idea for "The Adventure of the Single Footprint" came when I read an account of two books, entitled *Varieties of Temperament* and *Varieties of Human Physique,* by a Dr. Sheldon. The author had made the very interesting discovery that there is a distinct connection between one's physical appearance and one's temperament. To put it very simply, his findings showed that a short, fat man simply could not be similar in temperament to a tall, thin man. There were, of course, many more details than this, but he did say that by looking at a man he could fairly well predict his temperamental outlook.

It occurred to me that Sherlock Holmes would have found Dr. Sheldon's theories very interesting, and they might have helped him in some of his amazing deductions. Now, almost every mystery story writer wishes he could write a Sherlock Holmes story. I decided to pretend that a modern Sherlock

Holmes used Dr. Sheldon's theories to describe a criminal fully from just a single footprint.

The result was, after much hard work, "The Adventure of the Single Footprint." It is a rather tricky story and was very difficult to handle technically. I only wrote it because the idea appealed to me so much. However, it won a prize in a story competition conducted by Ellery Queen's Mystery Magazine.

One last word: as you will see on looking back at these stories, a great deal of characterization, background and action had to be added to the basic ideas. However, while much of this was the result of hard thinking, much of it also came more or less spontaneously as I was writing. There seems to be a little mechanism in the writer's mind that blends supplementary ideas together and feeds them to him without conscious thought once he gets started on a basic idea that interests him.

As you can see, story ideas come from many places and often quite unexpectedly.

About the Author

ROBERT ARTHUR, whose father was a colonel in the United States army, was born on the far-off island of Corregidor, in the Philippines. He attended William and Mary College and the University of Michigan, and received a Master of Arts degree from Michigan, where he majored in English.

For some years Mr. Arthur worked as a magazine editor, after which he turned to free-lance writing. He has written short stories, books, television and radio scripts, and has also been a story consultant for Alfred Hitchcock. Mr. Arthur lives in Cape May, New Jersey.